The Wife Finder

The Billionaires of Silicon Forest, Book One

MELISSA McCLONE

The Wife Finder
The Billionaires of Silicon Forest (Book 1)
Copyright © 2019 Melissa McClone

ALL RIGHTS RESERVED

Cover by Elizabeth Mackay

Cardinal Press, LLC
August 2019
ISBN-13: 9781944777371

Dedication

To Deb Bishko, Kent Williams, and Al Nash
BFFs • I love you guys • Go Cardinal!

Special thanks to:
Dan Niles, Jennifer Niles, Warren Niles, Mike Orsak,
Kent Williams, and Adaline Fraser for answering my
many questions. Artistic license taken. Any mistakes
are mine.

Chapter One

As the groom slid the garter from the bride's leg, guests cheered. Blaise Mortenson didn't join in. Instead, he rubbed the back of his neck and tried not to frown. A multimillion-dollar wedding at a winery in Oregon's Willamette Valley with performances by singers who graced the top of the Billboard charts and dinner prepared by a Michelin-star chef, yet the newlyweds had included every reception tradition pinned on Pinterest.

Given the bride was a successful event planner, he shouldn't be surprised. The groom's two-point-six-billion-dollar net worth meant everything tonight was over-the-top bespoke.

Blaise fought the urge to step outside and check his email. Better yet if he returned to his hotel room and his laptop.

But he couldn't.

His friends would never let him hear the end of it. And rightly so. Tonight was worth celebrating.

Three down, two to go.

Mason Reese saying "I do" today meant the social media app billionaire was out. He'd lost the bet. Surprising—okay, shocking—because he'd come up with the "last single man standing" wager five years ago.

Half of the six friends participating were now married. All within the past three months. Which was why as soon as Mason announced his engagement and wedding date, Blaise had stopped drinking the tap water in the Portland-metro area.

Crazy, yes, but he wasn't taking any chances. He even brushed his teeth with bottled water. Call him superstitious or paranoid, but something in the water would explain why his friends were falling in love and marrying so fast. Not that Blaise minded the rash of nuptials or having to purchase each couple a wedding gift.

Only two more to go until he won the bet.

He would be the last single man standing no matter what it took.

Losing wasn't an option.

His cell phone buzzed. He reached for it.

"The text can wait." Wes Lockhart pushed Blaise's hand away from his tuxedo pocket. Wes had added muscle to his frame which had thinned when he was sick. His hair was the longest it had been in two years. "It's time to join the others on the dance floor."

Blaise lowered his arm to his side. "What for?"

"Mason's going to toss the garter."

Blaise flinched. He took a step back. "No."

"Yes." Wes shot him the infamous suck-it-up look. That must be something they taught rich kids at prep school. "Mason expects you, me, and Dash to be out there. Best friends forever, remember?"

The amusement in Wes's eyes didn't stop Blaise from feeling his bow tie tighten around his neck, threatening to cut off the blood flow to his brain. Okay, not really, but the outdated garter toss tradition should have disappeared with the dotcom-bubble-crash. That, however, wasn't the only reason he didn't want to take part.

He raised his chin. "Mason won't notice. He can't see anyone except his bride."

"Heart eyes have blinded him, but this is what friends do for one another." Wes's gaze softened. "The same way you guys made sure someone was with me during my chemo treatments."

Blaise hadn't known what to expect being a chemo buddy, but he'd appreciated the time with Wes despite the reason he was there. "That was different."

"It's the same."

Maybe, except…

"Mason will aim for one of us." The words flew from Blaise's mouth. "Adam and Kieran did that at their receptions. And remember the rules? If each of us marries within a year of the first wedding, the bet is off. That's only nine months from now."

Blaise sounded like a kid on the verge of a tantrum, but he couldn't help himself. So much money was at stake he had to be careful. Sure, the six of them were wealthy. They weren't called the Billionaires of Silicon Forest—Oregon's version of the Bay Area's Silicon Valley—for nothing. But he wanted…more. Winning the five-hundred-million-dollar pot and bragging rights would help him reach his goals that much quicker. Normally, he allowed things to play out in due time, knowing the payoff would occur, but not with the bet. He felt compelled to make it happen. Sooner rather than later.

Wes laughed. "I can't believe a piece of lingerie is scaring the mighty, hard-nosed Blaise Mortenson."

"Not scared." Blaise's spine went ramrod stiff. "But Kieran caught the garter at Adam's wedding. Mason caught it at Kieran's. Whoever catches Mason's…"

Wes eyed him warily. "Last week, you claimed they fell in love because of the water."

Blaise shrugged. Not that he was indifferent or unsure. His ability to recognize patterns had made his company—and him—successful.

"The water. The garter. Who knows? But no need

to take chances." He would rather get poison ivy or the flu than catch the wisp of fabric soon to be tossed. "You go out there, I'm—"

"Coming with me."

Not about to budge, he squared his shoulders. "What about the Wonderkid?"

"Right here." Dashiell Cabot, AKA Dash, hurried toward them.

Taller than both Wes and Blaise, Dash pushed his light brown hair out of his eyes. His bow tie was crooked. So was his cummerbund. The guy was more comfortable in a hoodie and sweatpants. And until his company had brought in a high-level handler to teach Dash how to act like a CEO, that was all he'd worn— even to board meetings.

Known as the Wonderkid of Silicon Forest, Dash had founded a company in his freshman dorm room and dropped out of college before his junior year. Five years ago, just in time for their bet, he became a self-made billionaire at twenty-three. A few people called him Midas because whatever new data mining product he developed became that industry's gold standard. Dash had tackled insurance and military. Who knew what was next for him?

"I stepped outside to take a call," Dash explained. "There's a project milestone we need to reach, and someone had a question."

Wes blew out a breath. "There's more to life than working a hundred hours a week."

Yeah, right. Try one hundred and twenty, but Blaise didn't roll his eyes as he once might have. Wes didn't deserve that. "You used to do the same."

"Emphasis on used to," Wes said without missing a beat. "Cancer makes a person reassess his priorities."

"I'm sure it does." Blaise was grateful Wes was in remission. Until he'd gotten sick, Wes had worked more than Dash and Blaise combined. "But work is the most important thing in my life and always will be."

"Until you meet *the one*," Dash chimed in. "Then things will change."

Say what? That was the last thing Blaise expected to hear coming from the biggest nerd among them. Given they all had a few geek tendencies—though Wes not as much—that was saying something.

Wes's gaze snapped to Dash's. "What do you know about *the one?*"

"Nothing." Dash sounded as if that was an unusual position for him to be in. Given he was one of the smartest people on the planet, it probably was. "But each time I pull an all-nighter or spend the weekend at the office, everyone says that."

"It doesn't matter where you sleep," Blaise said in a matter-of-fact tone. He had a pullout couch in his office. Dash had a futon. "A bed is a bed."

"Exactly," Dash agreed. "Plus, people fail to understand I already found my one."

Wes's jaw dropped.

Blaise understood his surprise. Dash dated women who sought him out. The ones who didn't mind him working so much stuck around until they realized they'd never be more than someone to hang out with when he had free time, which wasn't often. "Who?"

Dash's grin lit up his face. "Zel—"

"Video game princesses don't count," Wes interrupted. The disdain on his face matched the tone of his voice.

Blaise laughed.

"Even if she's perfect?" Dash asked, sounding like a gaming-addicted teenager. Then again, he'd always been the baby of the group—age-wise and maturity level.

"Even then." Wes sounded older than thirty-five, but he'd always taken on the role of their big brother. "But if your new top-secret project involves general intelligence, we can revisit the princess being your one after you make a prototype of her."

Dash frowned as if his game controller had gone dead.

Wes laughed. "Given this discussion and the fact none of us are dating, the bet might drag on forever."

"What bet?" Dash asked.

This time Blaise couldn't stop rolling his eyes. "Last single man standing bet."

"Oh, right," Dash said. "I forgot."

Blaise's mouth fell open. "How could you forget?"

Dash shrugged. "I don't think about it. Or marriage. Or anything that isn't work-related. Unless it's—"

"A video game," Blaise and Wes said at the same time.

Wes motioned them toward the dance floor. Blaise begrudgingly went out there.

A drum roll played.

"Are all the single men on the dance floor?" a singer who had recently finished a world tour asked with a grating voice. She glanced around. Her eyes, caked with thick eyeliner and heavy mascara, lingered on him before doing the same to Wes and Dash.

Blaise's muscles tightened.

Typical.

Except most women only saw their net worth. Much of which was tied up in their respective companies or funds, in his case, but the term billionaire implied an extravagant lifestyle, one with an American Express "Black" card and a Visa "White" card. Few understood the work involved in running a successful company. The attention from gorgeous women used to be flattering to Blaise, who'd been bullied in school, a nerd who girls ignored. Now, he found most women who wanted to date him vapid— the definition of annoying.

The singer glanced at the groom who grinned like

a cat waiting for a second serving of canary. "Are you ready?"

Ready for another drink—a shot.

Tequila or whiskey, Blaise didn't care with the top-shelf liquor being poured by generous bartenders. A famous mixologist had been flown in from New York to create signature wedding cocktails.

Other men, however, whooped and hollered as if the outcome of their evening depended on catching the bride's garter.

Losers.

But they were welcome to it.

"Smiling won't kill you, Mortenson," Wes teased. "Wedding receptions are supposed to be fun."

"I was having fun until you made me come out here."

Even if Blaise wanted to argue about being forced to participate, he wouldn't. A few of his company's board of directors were here somewhere. They'd been on him about being nicer to his employees. Besides, Mason and his bride deserved better than Blaise causing a scene.

To appease Wes, Blaise forced the corners of his mouth upward in a move he'd perfected.

"Three, two, one..." the singer said into the microphone.

Mason shot the blue and white garter. It soared through the air on a direct trajectory toward...

Blaise cursed under his breath. His tuxedo-clad

shoulders sagged.

This had to be a setup.

Too bad because he wasn't playing.

He shoved the tips of his fingers into his pockets.

The garter hit his left lapel before dropping to the floor.

People gasped.

A few laughed.

Another snickered.

The drummer hit the cymbal.

He ignored them. Otherwise, he might be tempted to scoop up the blue silk and lace-trimmed garter lying across the toe of his patent-leather derby shoe.

Focus on winning the bet.

"Pick it up," Wes growled under his breath.

Blaise kept his hands in his pockets, but he glanced at Dash.

"Don't look at me." Dash held his hands in the air. "The garter is all yours."

On stage, Mason cleared his throat. Glared. His nostrils flared.

Okay, some action was required.

No worries. Blaise was a fix-it guy.

From his peripheral vision, he spotted a boy. Maybe four, maybe ten. Blaise had no idea how old. He avoided children, but this would solve his current problem.

Pulling his hands out of his pockets along with a

hundred-dollar bill from his money clip, he caught the kid's attention. With a flick of his wrist, Blaise raised the money slightly before pointing to the garter.

Excitement exploded in the kid's eyes. With the smoothness of a Wimbledon ball boy, he ran onto the dance floor, swooped up the garter, and grabbed the bill out of Blaise's hand.

Guests laughed and applauded with the doting parents looking on.

As the crowd quieted and men left the dance floor, Blaise pumped his fist.

Issue resolved. Crisis averted.

Time for that drink.

Eager to escape whatever lecture Wes wanted to give, Blaise wove his way around the linen-covered tables toward the bar.

Halfway there, Henry Davenport stepped in front of him. He was dressed in a burgundy tuxedo jacket, and his mouth twisted. "Nice show out there."

Henry reeked of old money, which he'd inherited after the deaths of his parents, but he didn't intimidate Blaise. "It worked out."

"For the kid. But Mason was aiming for you."

"Not my fault he did that," Blaise said with zero emotion in his voice. Henry was well-connected and close friends with Brett Matthews, who ran Matthews Global Investments and was someone Blaise respected. He needed to be nice and polite—what the board accused him of not being. "Mason should have aimed for Wes or Dash."

Henry raised his left brow. "Wes is trying to get his life back on track, and Dash is hopeless with relationships. That means you're the next in line to get married."

Uh-oh. Henry enjoyed playing matchmaker. His first successful match had occurred when he set up Brett and his wife, Laurel. Not that Blaise was a part of Henry's group. Portland might be the largest city in Oregon, but it wasn't *that* big of a town for those with money.

Blaise crossed his arms as if to ward off a vampire. Henry would happily suck the singleness out of him. "Mason knows I'm not interested in getting married."

"The garter toss is a tradition."

"Many brides and grooms opt to have an anniversary dance instead," Blaise countered.

"This couple chose otherwise yet you ruined the moment. *Their* moment."

"Hey." He didn't appreciate the accusation in Henry's voice. "I made that kid's day. He got the garter and a hundred-dollar bill. I call that a win."

Henry's lips parted. "This is about the bet."

"Yes." Blaise had no reason to lie.

Henry blew out a breath. "Catching the garter doesn't mean you're—"

"Not taking any chances." Blaise straightened. "I will win."

"You've said that before."

Confidence flowed through him. "It's true."

"There's more to life than winning."

Easy to say for a guy who'd been born into money and never had to work a day in his life. A man with parents who loved him and a mansion full of staff who made sure he was clean and fed and safe. Henry didn't know what going hungry was like. Or being left alone when Blaise's parents went off on a binge. Or sleeping under a box in the pouring rain because he was too afraid to be at home when his parents invited their druggie friends over.

"Like what?" he asked.

Henry scratched his cheek. He started to speak and then stopped himself.

Knew it. Blaise laughed. "Winning is everything."

"Godchildren."

"Excuse me?"

"Godchildren are better than winning," Henry explained. "Little Noelle is the most precious human to grace this earth. She will grow up to be president or win a Nobel Prize or do both."

Henry was known for his hyperbole, but no one could deny the guy's love for Brett and Laurel's daughter. Not that Blaise understood the infatuation. "Children are sticky and dirty. Their noses are always running. They don't know how to be quiet or sit still."

"Because they're kids."

"I'll stick to winning."

"Being in love is better than winning." Henry beamed with pride. "Or so I've been told."

"I wouldn't know." Blaise was too busy working to get wrapped up in a woman. Casually dating when he had time or wanted company was enough. "But I'll take winning over love any day. Saves me from paying lawyers to write an iron-clad prenup. Which is why I'm winning the bet."

Henry cocked a brow. "Wes and Dash might have something to say about that."

Neither man appeared interested in dating, but Blaise doubted the bet was the reason. At least not for Dash, who had forgotten about it until tonight. Wes, however, might care and be a worthy opponent. The man had decimated companies with his take-no-prisoner attitude to get where he was today—the wealthiest of the six. Bragging rights would mean more to him than the money. They were fifty-fifty for Blaise.

Winning was a way to prove he was one of them. That skinny kid, who qualified for free breakfast and lunch at school, lurked inside him, still hungered for acceptance, that ever-elusive sense of belonging, and security.

That was why Blaise needed to convince his two friends marriage was the best—the only option—they wanted to pursue. Seeing Henry gave Blaise an idea on how to make that happen.

"Want to play matchmaker?" he asked. "If anyone

could accomplish the task, you could."

Henry laughed. "Thanks for the compliment, but I promised Brett I would only play matchmaker on my birthday. April first is nearly seven months away. Unless you want to wait until then."

Blaise didn't have that much patience. Especially with so much money to be won. "I'll find someone else."

"If you want to hire an official matchmaker, I can recommend someone." Henry tilted his head. "They call her the wife finder."

"Sounds perfect since I need to find Wes and Dash wives."

"If anyone can help you do that, Hadley can. She works differently than other matchmakers, but she's the best around. I'll text you her number."

"Hadley?" Blaise asked.

"Hadley Lowell," Henry replied. "She lives in San Francisco and also has an office in New York. She's thorough. Discreet. Successful. And expensive."

"Sounds like she's exactly what I need."

"Oh, she definitely is."

Good. The sooner Blaise's friends fell in love and got married, the sooner he would be declared the winner.

Chapter Two

At 6:00 AM on Monday morning, Hadley Lowell placed three planners and a zippered pouch full of colored pens on the kitchen table. The scent of freshly brewed coffee filled the air of her two-bedroom condo in San Francisco's Marina District. She inhaled once, twice…

No caffeine, remember?

Instead of pouring herself a steaming cup of her favorite brand of coffee, she reached for the glass of water with half a lemon squeezed into it.

She sat at the table.

A week ago, Hadley had stopped drinking coffee after hearing lower caffeine intake improved sleep quality. She'd been so tired she went cold turkey. No coffee, tea, or chocolate. Since then, she not only tossed and turned in bed but was also jittery and yawning during the day.

Withdrawal symptoms?

She'd go one more week before adding caffeine back into her diet.

Hadley indulged herself with one more sniff before sipping her lemon water. She wished it hit the same spot as well as freshly ground dark-roasted coffee beans brewed and served with a dash of cream.

"Seriously?" Her younger sister, Fallon Caples, entered the kitchen. The heels of her pumps clicked against the hardwood, wide-plank floor. Her blond hair was pulled back in a tight ponytail. The severe style fit well with the lime green pencil skirt and coordinating jacket she'd purchased at a thrift shop. She was dressed to impress. Still, the tired circles and lines on her face made her look older than thirty-two. "It's too early on a Monday morning to pull out the planners. Especially when we went over everything last night."

Hadley opened the top one. "I want to review the kids' schedules so I don't forget something."

"You never forget anything." Fallon poured coffee into her *Best Mom Ever* mug. "I'm only out of town until Thursday. No need to plan out my absence like a military operation."

Except Hadley did that with every part of her life—personal and professional. Without schedules and plans, she would be lost. Or feel that way. Same difference to her. "This is what I do."

"Yes, but it's unnecessary." Fallon took a sip of coffee. "Skip the kids' activities this week."

Hadley gasped, tightening her grip on the pen. Just the thought... Her stomach churned. "Why would I do that?"

"Because you have a business to run. You should spend time with Audra and Ryder as their aunt, not their second parent, and have fun with them."

"We have fun. You guys make this place a home." A crowded one, especially with an overweight cat named Tiny who thought he was a dog, but Hadley was saving for a bigger place. Her parents had helped her purchase the condo, but her current goal was to sell it and buy a house in the same neighborhood so the kids—in first and second grade—wouldn't have to switch schools again. They'd previously been enrolled in a private school. Real estate in San Francisco was expensive, especially in the Marina District, so a move was a solid year, maybe two, away. "It's nothing like the house where you lived before..."

"This is better. Perfect. I don't know what we would do without you and this condo." Gratitude filled Fallon's voice. "You've sacrificed so much for us."

"We're family." The words shot out fast. Firm.

After the arrest of Fallon's husband, Hadley hadn't thought twice about taking in her sister and the kids. Their parents had retired early, sold everything, given them each money, and moved onto a cruise ship. They loved their new lifestyle, and though they visited and sent money if needed, they'd raised their family and wanted to travel.

Which was why her sister and the kids lived with Hadley now.

"You should be dating." Fallon refilled her cup. "Not being a stand-in parent for my two kids."

"I have all I need right here with you three." Hadley didn't want her sister to feel bad. Fallon had been through enough with her loser ex-husband. "Besides, we both know my amazing success rate finding my clients the loves of their lives hasn't translated to my own. I suck at finding myself a decent guy to date. Or…you."

Fallon waggled her index finger. "You introduced me to Clint, but he wasn't one of your clients and neither was I."

Guilt coated Hadley's throat. "I—"

"Stop." As Fallon's eyes narrowed, her lips tightened into a thin line. "I take full responsibility for falling for his lies and marrying him. There were plenty of warning signs I ignored. What happened is on me. You've gone above and beyond by taking us in and finding me a job."

"It's…"

Not enough.

"Everything." Fallon's lips curved upward. For a

moment, she appeared a decade younger and ready to take on the world. Not a harried single mom with two kids, all her assets confiscated, and an ex-husband who would spend the next twenty years in jail for embezzlement and fraud. "And when I'm ready, though it might take me a few more years to get to that point, I'll even ask you to fix me up with a nice, honest man who wouldn't mind taking on a ready-made family and cat."

Hadley's mouth dropped open. "You want to get married again?"

Fallon raised her chin. "I liked being married. Clint wouldn't win any husband- or father-of-the-year awards, but I can't assume every man is the same. Besides, without him, I wouldn't have the two greatest kids in the world."

"That's…"

"Stupid?"

"Mature." More so than Hadley was with dating. One bad relationship after another had soured her on romance. She'd given up to focus on her clients. If anything, her sister and the kids gave Hadley a valid excuse why she wasn't in the market for a boyfriend. Or a date. "I'm proud of you."

"Thank you. I'm trying to look for the silver lining in what happened. Including spending this week in Los Angeles."

"Even though you'll be working, the trip will be good for you. No sharing a bedroom or a bathroom."

"Or nighttime calls for a glass of water." Fallon smiled. "But I'm not the only one who needs to get away. You haven't taken a vacation in over a year."

Hadley shrugged. "I'm at the New York office twice a month."

"Still work."

She was about to say she caught a Broadway show or a performance at the Met when she was there, but she hadn't done that since Fallon and the kids moved in. "But I'm working in the Big Apple. That has to count for something."

According to one recent survey, San Francisco had the highest number of billionaires per capita. New York was second. That was why she had offices in both cities. Not that she only worked with billionaires. Anyone who wanted to pay her fee and did as she required was welcome. Seeing her clients live happily ever after was almost as good as the money she made. Emphasis on almost. Still, no one could argue with her success rate. None of the couples matched by her firm had divorced since she opened her business seven years ago.

She wanted a perfect match for her sister, too. Audra and Ryder deserved a dad—a loving, kind, honest father.

Speaking of which…

"Okay, the kids." Hadley grabbed the yellow pen—the color for her niece's activities. "Let's start with Audra."

Fallon rolled her eyes. "You are anal retentive, OCD, and a control freak."

"Yet you still love me."

"I do." Fallon sat and placed her mug on the table. "If not for those tendencies, you wouldn't be as successful as you are and the kids and I would be—"

"Wherever I was."

Therapy was helping the three with trust and abandonment issues. Hadley had her own issues after past relationships left her feeling used and worthless. They were one big happy family trying to lighten their emotional baggage.

"I'm not going anywhere," she added, hoping to put her sister at ease. Hadley readied her pen. "So Audra…"

"Dance today. Choir on Tuesday. Nothing on Wednesday. And soccer on Thursday."

Hadley had written those. She picked up the red pen. "Now Ryder."

"Soccer game today, nothing on Tuesday, soccer on Wednesday, and a piano lesson on Thursday." Fallon raised her mug. "No playdates scheduled. Both kids keep mentioning that story time you took them to and want to go back."

That had been a fun Saturday. The three of them had gone out to breakfast before hitting Cassandra's Attic, a local bookstore. "I'll see what the shop has coming up."

"This week is full." Fallon's mouth slanted.

"Don't make more work for yourself."

"A bookstore is the definition of fun."

"If you think that, then you need a boyfriend. And not a book one. A real-life, blood-flowing-through-his-veins, kisses-you-until-your-toes-curl boyfriend."

As if those existed.

Not in Hadley's world. Book boyfriends were safer. They didn't disappoint her the way real men had.

She stuck her tongue out at her sister.

Fallon did the same.

Hadley laughed. "Better not let the kids see us, or they'll copy."

"Too late. They started as soon as they discovered that appendage in their mouths." Fallon motioned to the planners. "Anything else you want to discuss?"

One planner contained the menu plan, but Hadley had filled that out before the month began. It saved running to the grocery store because they didn't have what they needed to make dinner. The other planner held her budget. Hadley didn't want to bring that up because Fallon hated discussing money. Her sister had gone from spending whatever she wanted to watching every dollar she spent and cutting coupons.

"I'm good," Hadley said. "I keep the three together so I know where everything is."

Fallon giggled, a sound that wasn't as rare as it had been a few months ago. Another sign that she was healing, albeit slowly. "I'm so tempted to rearrange the sheets in your planner and watch you freak out."

Hadley grabbed the three planners and clutched them against her chest. Her pulse raced. The discs holding the pages together would make it easy for someone to mix up the pages or remove some without her knowing.

She took a breath and then another. "That would be cruel."

Humor glinted in Fallon's eyes. "You know I'm joking."

Yes, but that didn't stop a shiver from racing along Hadley's spine. When they were kids, she remembered the horror when Fallon had cut off the hair on Hadley's favorite doll.

Maybe she would store the planners in her desk.

And lock it from now on.

That way Fallon wouldn't be tempted…

* * *

An hour later, Hadley entered the lobby of the workspace floor where she leased a two-person office. Companies like this were the hottest trend across the country, allowing businesses flexibility with their office space, and giving her a popular business location for an affordable price.

Her computer bag hung from her shoulder,

bouncing against her hip. The scent of coffee tempted her, but she ignored it.

"Good morning, Hadley," a receptionist greeted her with a wide smile. "Ella dropped off today's list of appointments. We'll take good care of your clients."

"Thanks."

A short walk down a hallway and two right turns later, she opened the door to her office. A familiar sense of pride washed over her—the same way it did each morning when she stepped inside.

Some people called her the wife finder. Others the husband finder. She was fine with either moniker. Her clientele came from word of mouth. The more people talked about her services, the better for her business.

"You're early this morning." Ella, her assistant, greeted her. "Getting the kids off to school must have gone smoothly."

"It did." Hadley approached the desk. "Ryder misplaced a shoe, but it was under the couch so it didn't take long to find."

"Good."

Yes, except... She studied her assistant. Hair, makeup, jewelry, and Ella's posture were perfect as always, but something was missing. A big something. "You're not smiling."

Ella shrugged.

Not a good sign.

Neither were the lines creasing her forehead,

emphasized by her intricate cornrow braids. The woman dressed to impress, coordinating in ways that would make paid stylists drool. Her competence and intelligence made her the best assistant ever. Her only flaw—if it could even be called that—was her kindness. Ella exuded compassion and empathy. Sometimes too much.

But Hadley didn't mind being the heavy if Ella couldn't do that on a phone call or in person.

Hadley mentally reviewed the list of current clients, but no red flags popped up. Not even yellow ones. She didn't work with people who caused problems. That was part of the reason for her high success rate. She limited the variables so less could go wrong. She knew each client's wants, needs, avoid lists by heart. Technology provided the first step in comparing profiles, but the matches came from a gut feeling telling her which two people belonged together.

She sat on the edge of Ella's desk. "What's up?"

"I've had three calls from a CEO's assistant. Each one was more frantic than the last. He'd left a message before I arrived this morning." Ella bit off what lipstick remained. "His boss wants to meet with you this afternoon in Portland, Oregon."

"Today?"

Worry filled Ella's brown-eyed gaze, stealing away the warmth that usually resided there. She nodded once. "Sounds like the boss isn't the type to take no for an answer."

None of these wealthy, successful types were. That was why Hadley had developed her own process to weed through potential clients. She didn't have as big a business as she could, but her market was niche. Matching couples to go on a date might be the starting point, but the end goal was to find a client the person they wanted to be with forever. Her services didn't end until they said "I do."

Some who came to her, however, weren't interested in falling in love. Finding a life partner wasn't their goal. They wanted a trophy—the definition of trophy depended on whether someone wanted arm candy or accomplished or both—a wife or a husband who fell at their feet without them having to put any effort into the relationship. Someone who would sign a prenup without complaint and be as pliant once wed. A spouse who would be nothing more than the newest addition to their portfolio of stocks, homes, and artwork. One they could show off until the time came to replace them with a younger version.

Which Clint had been planning to do to Fallon before his arrest.

Hadley turned down those people, telling them her services weren't a good fit. She only took on clients who wanted more.

Wanted love.

Wanted forever.

Those men and women were more flexible, willing to give up some control to find their perfect matches. Some complained loudly about what she expected from them, which she understood. Ultimately, without fail, each client who met her requirements had put or was putting in the effort required. The result—marriage. Given the nonexistent divorce rate so far, she would say a happy marriage. Each successful coupling gave her a glimmer of hope there was someone for everyone, especially Fallon. Even if logically Hadley had doubts about finding that herself.

Ella's missing smile made sense to Hadley now. "You're worried about the assistant."

"His boss sounds…demanding. Harsh. A bit of a jerk."

That wasn't a client Hadley wanted to take on. "Where do things stand after your last call?"

A sheepish expression flitted across Ella's face. "Whether he makes the flight reservation or I do?"

Hadley wasn't upset, but she needed Ella to be firmer with potential clients. Especially possible jerks. "*No* isn't a four-letter word."

"He said he would be fired if you didn't show up." Ella's voice cracked.

"Assistants always say that." Hadley smiled at Ella. "As soon as anyone hears your voice, they know you're a softy."

"Not *that* soft." Ella showed off her bicep. "At

least not anymore. I've lost twenty pounds and am working out at the gym now."

"Good for you." Hadley needed to do the same. And would. If she ever had any free time to exercise. At least she ate healthier now because of the kids. "But you're way friendlier to people, including strangers, than I am. That's why everyone likes you more than they like me."

"They don't." Ella's words shot out fast, but they lacked conviction.

"Yes, they do. And I don't mind."

Hadley was a business owner, not vying for a congeniality award. She wouldn't call herself standoffish, but she kept a comfortable distance from her clients, never mixing business with pleasure. She'd learned that lesson at a previous job.

"Did you explain my procedure for taking on a new client?" she asked.

"Yes. I also emailed him the info packet." Ella blew out a breath.

"I hear a *but* coming."

"But he said his boss didn't have time to do all that."

Of course, he said that because bosses never did. But finding love was something they had to make time for if they wanted her help. Guess this "boss" didn't.

Not a problem.

"You handled everything correctly once again."

Ella shrugged. "I didn't tell him to find another matchmaker."

The words sank in. "Why not?"

"His boss is Blaise Mortenson." She sounded impressed. "I know you don't like to bend the rules—"

"I don't bend rules. Ever." If Hadley hadn't become a matchmaker, her father said she would have been the perfect five-star army general.

"The assistant's name is Trevor. He's a new hire, who hasn't had the job for a month. He doesn't want to be fired."

"Even if he is, it's not your fault."

Ella stared at her monitor and nodded.

"Blaise Mortenson." Hadley rolled the name through her mind. A little familiar, but no details sprang to mind. That told her he probably wasn't marriage material, no matter his net worth. "Remind me who he is."

"He's the founder and CEO of Blai$e. It's spelled with a dollar sign for the S. Financial sector. Multibillion-dollar investment funds. Hi-tech algorithms. His last known net worth…" Ella leaned closer to her monitor. "One point two billion dollars. But that's an old figure."

Blai$e.

Hadley knew exactly who he was.

Unfortunately.

His attitude—well, that of his assistant, Trevor—

didn't surprise her.

She'd never met Blaise, but she'd researched him as a possible match for a client over a year ago.

Blaise Mortenson was gorgeous and self-made, which was usually a good thing, except he had an ego the size of Oregon, where he lived. He also had a reputation of being a difficult boss. He'd been in the news recently because of an exodus of high-level employees, including programmers. That had led to a heated run-in between Blaise and a reporter.

Hadley didn't know if the guy's anger issues, arrogance, or stress had caused the argument, but Blaise's actions didn't impress her. If anything, they reaffirmed her initial research. Forget his request to travel to him—not that she did that for anyone. He wasn't the kind of client she wanted. But even so, she needed to be polite if he called.

Or made an appointment with her.

She stood. "If Trevor calls again…"

As if on cue, the phone rang.

"Transfer the call to me if it's him." Hadley needed to turn Ella's frown into a smile. "And don't worry. I know this isn't the assistant's fault. I'll be pleasant."

And Hadley would. The guy couldn't help it if he worked for an egotistical jerk. She gave him points for trying to follow orders.

Even if he had no chance of doing what his boss asked.

Chapter Three

Blaise entered his office and left the door ajar. No one would make it past his new assistant. Trevor was twenty-five, energetic, and eager to please, but he had much to learn about being an executive assistant. Not surprising though, since he'd been in the position for only three weeks. That, however, was two weeks longer than his predecessor, so Blaise was hopeful the guy would work out.

He loosened his tie.

What was the name of the other one?

Sheila.

No, Siobhan.

She'd spent more time crying in the bathroom than sitting at her desk. Blaise didn't care about her being "highly sensitive." This was a high-pressure environment, not preschool. Sometimes people, including him, raised their voices and yelled. It wasn't personal. Simply business. Siobhan must have realized she wasn't cut out for the job because she quit before he could fire her.

So far Trevor hadn't cried. He'd come close last Thursday. On Friday, too. But Monday was a new day.

A brand-new week, as a matter of fact.

Too bad it was only eight forty in the morning and not Friday night.

Blaise yawned.

The comfortable couch called to him, but he sat at his desk.

He set the alarm on his cell phone, rested his elbows on his desk, cradled his head, and closed his eyes. The darkness and quiet soothed the thoughts pounding in his brain. He called the brief periods of rest nano-naps. They helped him stay alert all day, especially when he arrived before the markets opened in New York.

Blaise inhaled, filling his lungs to capacity before exhaling through his mouth. That didn't relieve the tension knotting the cords at the back of his neck. But he continued the breathing until...

Beep-beep-beep.

He startled. Opened his eyes. Straightened.

As he shut off the alarm, he noticed the time. Almost nine. He'd managed a few minutes of sleep, but he still felt wiped out. Far from typical for a Monday, but he hadn't expected to be chastised for forty minutes by two board members this morning.

Stop micromanaging.

Let go of control.

Be nicer.

Smile.

Compliment people.

Attend an anger management course.

Blaise's muscles tightened. They acted like he went on rampages with his staff. He didn't or hadn't. Yes, he expected hard work. Of course, he raised his voice, as needed. More than once he'd lost his temper. So had others in similar positions.

Well, everyone except Dash.

Nothing phased the Wonderkid.

Blaise wanting to know what was going on with a project shouldn't be a big deal. This was *his* company. One privately held and making people an obscene amount of money. But the only thing the Board of Directors wanted to oversee these days was him.

Which was ridiculous.

His employees were fortunate to work at Blai$e. So what if he didn't sing "Kumbaya" with them every day? Or put on a cheery morning meeting, AKA "*asa no chorei*," as they did in Japan?

That wasn't his style.

But he did what he could—and listened to the HR department's recommendations—to keep his employees healthy and happy with extra days off and every on-site benefit known to tech employees on the West Coast. Not to mention giving yearly bonuses at Christmastime based on profits. Last spring's move into a state-of-the-art corporate headquarters allotted dedicated space for mental health experts, ergonomic specialists, massage therapists, and personal trainers. He'd brought in experts on drug abuse, which had become an issue for companies because of the long hours, workload, and stress. The private gym rivaled commercial ones. Chefs provided healthy food and beverages to keep workers from relying on a steady diet of energy drinks and junk food.

But why wasn't that enough?

Blaise balled his hands.

The board didn't care what he did for employees. They wanted to focus on Blaise.

His failings. *His* faults. *His* flaws.

As if they'd been the ones who created a business in a studio apartment with one employee—him—and turned it into a top investment company with three hundred thirteen employees and billions invested with them. He doubted any of the board members even knew the exact number of people who worked at Blai$e as of this morning.

He did, because HR kept him posted, at his request. They were still down a few after the fiasco last month.

A knock sounded before Trevor peeked his head

inside the office and then entered. "I rescheduled your four o'clock."

"Thank you." See? Blaise could be polite. "What time does the matchmaker arrive?"

Trevor shifted his weight between his feet. He rubbed his lips together.

"Is there a problem?" Blaise asked.

"She's not coming." The words rushed out one on top of the other.

That was unexpected. Most people did as he asked. She did run a business—maybe she couldn't clear her schedule today. "What time does she arrive tomorrow?"

Trevor opened his mouth before closing it. He flexed his hands. "She doesn't travel to meet with clients."

Except Blaise wasn't a typical client. "Did you mention who I am?"

"Yes, sir."

"And that money was no object?"

"Yes, sir. That didn't matter to her."

Not true. Everyone had a price. Blaise would have to discover hers. Henry had said she was in San Francisco.

Less than a two-hour flight.

Winning the bet was a priority, but the board was on his back. He had meetings and conference calls scheduled. A new fund was set to debut. Even if he had a trip planned to the Bay Area… "Not doable."

Trevor raised his chin. "That's what I told Ms. Lowell."

The pride in his voice brought a smile to Blaise's face. The guy might have potential. "What did she say?"

"She, um, suggested you find another matchmaker."

Blaise's jaw dropped. "Was she joking?"

"Afraid not."

No one except his closest friends would dare say something like that to him. He didn't mind big egos. He respected those who put a value on their knowledge and skills, but this woman's response implied rigidity and told him she wasn't the right matchmaker for the job. He would happily hire someone else and give them a bonus on top of their usual fee. "Let's take her suggestion. Put together a list of other matchmakers."

"Ms. Lowell's assistant emailed me one."

Seriously? Blaise nearly laughed. He doubted the woman would stay in business long with those kinds of tactics and such poor customer service. Not his problem. He'd wasted too much time on this already.

"Research each name." He adjusted his tie. "I want to hire the person with the highest success rate."

Trevor stared at the carpet. Lines appeared around his mouth.

"Something wrong?" Blaise asked.

"It's just..." Trevor wrung his hands. "I looked

up the people on her list."

"And?"

"They're excellent, highly rated, but…" Trevor swallowed, his Adam's apple bobbing. "Ms. Lowell's success rate is unmatched in the industry. She mentioned that to me when she explained her process—"

"I don't care how she works. I'm only interested in results."

"Her process is how she gets results. First comes a questionnaire. Then she conducts face-to-face meetings with potential clients. After that, there are tests and surveys. She seems quite thorough." Trevor sounded impressed.

Blaise wasn't. But if she was the best, he would put up with her pride, and no doubt, arrogance given her ease at turning away prospective clients. "Are you sure she understood how much I'm willing to pay for her services?"

Trevor nodded. "She told me she makes no exceptions. The only way to hire her is to fill out the paperwork and make an appointment with her in San Francisco or New York."

Blaise scratched his chin, his fingers brushing over short whiskers. Henry Davenport wouldn't have recommended Hadley Lowell unless he believed she was the right person for the job. The guy might not want to settle down himself, but he was a romantic at heart. At least where friends were involved. He would want Wes and Dash to marry their perfect matches and be happy. As did Blaise. That meant hiring the best person.

He glanced at the time on his computer monitor. "Get Ms. Lowell on the phone."

Trevor stiffened. "Now?"

Blaise nodded once. "I don't have much time until my next meeting."

But it shouldn't take him long to convince her to change her mind. He would find her price and pay it.

Trevor hurried out of the office.

A minute later, the office phone on Blaise's desk buzzed. He picked it up. "Hello."

"Good morning, Mr. Mortenson. It's Hadley Lowell." Her voice was strong and full of confidence. "Trevor said you wanted to talk."

Blaise hadn't expected her to sound so young. The only things he knew about matchmakers were from movies. They were usually older women and a little quirky. Though voices could be ageless.

"I do," he replied. "Thanks for taking my call."

"What do you wish to discuss, Mr. Mortenson?"

He appreciated how she didn't mince words, but he wanted to take control. That meant slowing down the conversation even if time was money. "Please, call me Blaise."

A beat passed. And another.

"What can I do for you, Blaise?" she asked.

It wasn't lost on him that she hadn't told him to

call her Hadley. His position and wealth impressed people. She, however, didn't appear to be. His respect for her inched up.

He would get right to the point as she had. "I want to hire you."

"Thank you." Her tone was sincere. "But I spoke with Trevor about my requirements. He said you couldn't meet with me."

"It's true." Unfortunately.

He knew nothing about the woman on the other end of the phone beyond what Henry and Trevor had said, yet she intrigued Blaise. He wanted to know what made her expect so much of her clients. Stubbornness, self-worth, something else? Saying no to an assistant was easy, but would she also tell him no? He wanted to find out.

"My schedule is full, so I don't have time to travel right now."

"Finding true love is never a rush job or something that happens 'right now.' When I say process, I mean just that."

"I understand." Even if he didn't like it.

"I alternate weeks between my offices in San Francisco and New York. I meet with potential clients at both locations, if your future schedule allows for that."

Funny—or maybe not—Hadley sounded as if she knew he wouldn't be able to travel to her yet didn't care. Giving him an unworkable option was something he'd pulled on people in the past.

"It doesn't," he admitted. "If you would please make an exception—"

"I don't make exceptions." The words came out staccato. "My assistant sent Trevor a list of other matchmakers. Hire one of them."

Her directness caught him off guard. Something that didn't happen often. "I want you."

"Why is that?" Curiosity edged each word.

"You're the best."

She laughed, the sound seeping inside him in an unexpected but not entirely unwelcome way. "I am good at what I do."

No modesty. Blaise shouldn't be impressed, but he was.

Again.

"Which is why I can work the way I do," she added. "The matchmakers I recommended can help you so it won't impact your schedule."

Hadley Lowell was closing the door. Her tone and words told him that.

Blaise wasn't going away that easily. "I'm positive we can work out an arrangement that's beneficial for both of us. Time-wise for me and financially for you."

Silence filled the line.

She was probably checking her calendar. Satisfaction flowed through him. He leaned back in his chair.

"Your assistant mentioned that."

"I'm re-mentioning it. I'm a wealthy man, Ms. Lowell. I want to hire you, but I need you to come to me. To Portland." His arrogance was showing, but he didn't care. "Name your price."

Blaise had thrown down the gauntlet. The amount could be anything; he didn't care. Winning the bet was that important to him.

"As I told Trevor, I don't travel to meet potential clients." Her voice was more forceful. Almost…hard. "I wish you the best with your search."

"Money—"

"Won't change my mind. That's all I have to say on the matter, but I would like to mention something."

This might be the opening Blaise needed. "I'm listening."

She inhaled as if suddenly remembering she needed to breathe. "Trevor mentioned he's only been your assistant for a short time. Please know he did what you asked of him. This is how I work with all potential clients, no matter where they are located or their net worth."

Blaise waited for her to say she was sorry. He deserved an apology for the way she acted.

"Is there anything else you wanted?" she asked.

"How do you stay in business?" The words came out before he could stop them. But he wasn't sorry he'd asked the question.

She laughed again, only this time the sound

irritated him. "Because I'm the best at what I do. My process may appear peculiar to you, but those willing to meet me halfway get the results they desire."

"You don't meet anyone halfway."

"True." She paused. "I've found if a potential client isn't willing to follow my procedures and come to me, he or she isn't a good fit for my services."

He flinched. "You don't think I'd be a good fit."

"I didn't say that."

"If I came to you?"

"You're too busy, but I..." A keyboard clicked. "I have an opening tomorrow morning at nine. Someone needed to reschedule. My next opening after that is in December."

Whoa. That was three months away.

"Could we hold the meeting online?" he asked. "I can have Trevor set up everything. All you'd need to do is log on."

"The meeting must be in person. I can learn more about someone face-to-face."

She was not only rigid but also inflexible. Which was what the board accused him of being.

Except Blaise wasn't. He just had work to do.

His hours weren't set. He could fly to the Bay Area and arrange a meeting or two so it wouldn't be a complete loss of time, but he didn't want to do that. She was asking too much. He'd stopped jumping through other people's hoops years ago. "I can't because of prior obligations."

"Then there's nothing more for us to discuss. I wish you success. Good luck, Blaise."

The line disconnected before he could reply.

He stared at the phone in disbelief.

Who was this woman?

No matter. Blaise set his phone on the desk.

Her loss.

He would hire someone equally good or better. He called Trevor who picked up after the first ring. "I want you to dig deep into each matchmaker on the list. Put together the top two or three for me to interview."

"Ms. Lowell said no." Trevor didn't sound surprised.

"The travel is a deal-breaker for her." As it was for Blaise. "Stop whatever else you've been doing. This is your priority."

"Yes, sir."

When his mom wasn't high or desperate for a fix, she used to say everything happened for a reason. Another matchmaker was out there. Blaise would find the right one.

Because Wes and Dash deserved only the best.

* * *

I can't believe I'm in San Francisco.

Four hours after his call with Hadley Lowell, Blaise flexed his fingers, trying to release the tension bunching his muscles. He battled a growing frustration. Since leaving the office, he'd spent every minute working or on the phone so he wouldn't fall further behind because of this unexpected trip.

He blamed Trevor.

I haven't worked for you long, Blaise, but if you want to find a wife, you need to hire Ms. Lowell. My gut and my research tell me that. She'll get the job done right.

Whether his assistant showed bravery or stupidity by speaking up remained to be seen, but Trevor had been so earnest that Blaise had gone against his better judgment and flown to San Francisco. His schedule was irregular. Even though he paid others to woo clients and recruits, there were times he'd dropped everything to do his part. So this wasn't totally unprecedented.

His desire to win the bet sooner rather than later had provided the real motivation. Knowing he couldn't win on his own, however, somehow made being here worse. He was used to doing everything himself and hated needing help. That had made seeking investors in the start-up days of Blai$e difficult for him on several levels.

The elevator dinged. The doors opened.

Before he could exit, two men in suits stepped to the left, leaving a much wider path than necessary. That was because of the guy standing next to Blaise— his bodyguard.

Lex's short, bleach-blond hair harkened back to

his military days, but it was his intense gaze, the scar on his face, and hard expression that kept people away from Blaise.

Which was the point.

Lex exited first, surveyed the area, and motioned Blaise to follow.

Blaise doubted anyone was waiting to ambush him, especially in the Bay Area where billionaires—many worth more than him—were everywhere, but he had no choice. Ever since the fight with that business reporter, he'd been accompanied by a member of the security team contracted by his company.

Lex opened the door where Hadley Lowell leased an office. "You okay, boss?"

No. Blaise wasn't, but he kept his feelings to himself. A lesson he'd learned at a young age.

"Fine." Although he would need a massage when he returned home. He rubbed the back of his tight neck. "Sorry you drew the short straw and had to come with me."

"That's why I'm paid the big bucks." Lex laughed. "I prefer assignments like this."

Most days Blaise's assigned person did nothing other than see him to the office and back home. He could have easily come here on his own without worry, but his company now required him to travel with at least one bodyguard. "Must be boring when you're stuck waiting for me to finish working."

Lex shrugged. "Better than being shot at."

Maybe boring wasn't so bad.

"And San Francisco holds a special place in my heart after an assignment here," Lex added.

The man didn't offer more information, and Blaise knew better than to ask. He went up to the front desk where two sharply dressed receptionists sat. "I'm here to see Hadley Lowell."

"Do you have an appointment?" one asked.

"She's not expecting me until tomorrow." Not exactly the truth, but Blaise needed to see her. He flashed his most charming smile, the one he used to soothe ruffled investors and captivate supermodels. "I took an earlier flight."

The receptionist didn't appear impressed. "What's your name?"

"Blaise." He paused, mimicking his favorite secret agent. "Blaise Mortenson."

The receptionist did a double take. Her mouth dropped open.

The other one gasped.

A billionaire seeking out a matchmaking company might have that effect. Especially if these two women were single.

"Oh. We don't want to ruin the surprise." The first woman stood. "Ms. Lowell's office is down the hall. Take the first two rights. Or I'm happy to show you—"

"Thanks, but I can find it." Turning toward Lex,

Blaise tilted his head toward the couches and chairs on the other side of the lobby. "Wait there."

Lex studied the area. "Sure, boss."

As Blaise headed toward the hallway, his cell phone buzzed. He glanced at his screen and was surprised to see a text from Henry.

Henry: *You made the right choice flying to SF.*
Blaise: *How do you know where I am?*
Henry: *I have my ways. Hadley Lowell is exactly who you need.*
Blaise: *She better be, given what she's putting me through.*
Henry: *Trust me.*
Blaise: *If you're wrong…*
Henry: *I won't be.*

Blaise stopped in front of a door with a small, blink-and-miss-it sign: *Matched by Lowell.*

Low-key. Not flashy.

The subtle branding didn't match the woman's demanding requirements. He would have expected something more on point for her industry. She better be as good as Henry said or…

The door opened, startling Blaise.

A woman stepped into the doorway. She was four inches shorter than him with auburn shoulder-length hair, ivory skin, and pink cheeks. Early to mid-thirties. And gorgeous.

Mouthwateringly so.

She wasn't one of those women who were so thin their heads look out of proportion, the kind who only ate salad and an occasional slice of avocado toast. That type didn't appeal to him. This one did. She had curves—nice ones.

Blaise wanted to memorize every detail.

Her blue eyes reminded him of the sky on a summer day, when flowers bloomed, the sun shone, and the dark, lonely nights didn't last as long as they did in winter.

He stared transfixed, connected to this stranger by an invisible force. Awareness thrummed through him. Staring was rude, but he couldn't look away from her.

Noises sounded. Muted footsteps. A door. A phone.

All Blaise could focus on was her.

Maybe this trip hadn't been such a bad idea. He couldn't remember the last time he'd been so…captivated.

She blinked. "Can I help you?"

Her voice was deeper than expected, a tad husky. Sexy. He wanted to hear her say more. He bet she had a great laugh.

She cleared her throat. "You're Blaise Mortenson."

The woman didn't sound surprised. If anything, she appeared resigned.

Did that mean…?

Of course, it did. "You're Hadley Lowell."

She nodded once.

His insides deflated. A strange reaction. One he would ignore.

Hadley eyed him curiously. "I thought you were too busy to come to San Francisco."

"Yes, but you're the best matchmaker, so here I am."

"I told you my next appointment is tomorrow at nine."

"That was before I changed my plans." And asked Trevor to cancel calls and reschedule meetings. Blaise needed to be in his office before the markets opened tomorrow. "Let's talk now."

She locked the door to the office before facing him again. "That won't work."

"I'm here. I came to you. As you require." Something he normally wouldn't have done. For anyone. Then again, he usually wouldn't notice the cute freckles sprinkled across the bridge of her nose. "Can't you be a little flexible?"

Hadley's jaw tensed. "You're not the only one with obligations."

"I'll make it worth your while."

Her face scrunched. "Does throwing money at a problem always work for you?"

"Usually."

"Not this time." She adjusted the strap of her computer bag. "I have to go."

"Wait." Blaise hadn't blocked Hadley's way, but he didn't want her to leave yet. The last commercial flight to Portland departed at eleven tonight. He wanted to be on it, because this visit wasn't worth the carbon footprint of a private jet ride. "Are you free this afternoon or this evening? I can meet you no matter what time you have available."

"Mr. Mortenson—"

"Blaise."

She frowned. "Blaise, I have two children to pick up from school in less than forty-five minutes. After that, we have a busy afternoon planned."

Children?

Disappointment shot through him.

A glance at her left hand showed a bare ring finger. That meant she was divorced or widowed. For some odd reason, the realization brought relief. "How old are your kids?"

"They're my niece and nephew." Hadley's knuckles turned white around her keys. "Both are young enough I can't keep them waiting. So if you'll excuse me—"

"I'll go with you."

Her brows furrowed. "What did you say?"

Her question took him aback because he'd said the first thing that had come to his mind. "I'll come with you."

"Why would you want to do that?"

He wasn't ready to say goodbye. No, that wasn't

the reason. He was here to discuss her matchmaking service so he could win the bet. "I'm sure you'll have a block of free time so we can talk."

She half laughed. "You don't have children."

The thought of loud, sticky small humans made him squirm. "No."

"Have you spent much time around children?"

Donating money to charities that helped kids was fine, but real-life interactions? He shuddered. "No."

Hadley rubbed her mouth. "It'll be easier if you wait until tomorrow morning."

"I can't wait. This is important to me."

A door opened down the hall.

She glanced that way before looking at him. "What if we don't have time to talk?"

Now she was making excuses, trying to get out of meeting with him, but he wouldn't let her off that easily.

Wes was the image of smooth and eloquent no matter the situation. Adam and Kieran weren't as charming, but they held their own. Dash could be the poster child for introverted, socially clueless tech guys. Mason was a step above him. Blaise, however, fell in the middle of his friends.

On purpose.

He hated meaningless chitchat, but he'd realized the ability to mingle and make small talk would help him get ahead. It wasn't something that came naturally, but that hadn't stopped him. He'd observed and practiced. He had a feeling those lessons would come in handy with Hadley.

Blaise would keep his voice light. "I wouldn't blame you."

"I hope not, since it wouldn't be my fault."

Okay, maybe his tone hadn't been as playful as he'd hoped, but hiding his irritation was harder than he thought it would be. She was the problem. Not him. If she were more flexible with her process, this trip to San Francisco wouldn't have been necessary.

"Can I come along?" he asked in his this-will-be-fun voice he used when an overnight shift debugging code faced his team. He would try one more thing. "Please."

She blew out a breath. "Let's go."

Blaise fought the urge to pump his fist. Instead, he fell in step next to her as she headed to the lobby at a quick pace.

"Do you have a car?" he asked.

She held up her keys. "I do."

Guess he wouldn't need the SUV, except… "Lex can follow us."

"Who is Lex?"

"One of my bodyguards."

"The more the merrier." Her tone was more ominous than humorous. "But if you think we'll have a meeting in bits and pieces while I drive, ride with Lex."

Blaise held up his hands, palms out. "I can wait

until we have a block of time."

"You might be waiting awhile." She eyed him warily. "Don't say I didn't warn you."

No worries. He'd shown up unexpectedly and asked her to make an exception for their meeting. But that was what he did—tackled issues head-on.

No one got the better of him.

Especially a matchmaker, one who thought she was in control on her home turf.

She wasn't.

Blaise would let her get the children settled into whatever activity or routine the kids had then they would have their meeting. He would answer her questions, pay her retainer fee, and then go to the airport. He might even make an earlier flight.

He was happy he'd listened to Trevor and Henry.

This would work out...perfectly.

Chapter Four

As Hadley drove toward the kids' school, she clutched the Outback's steering wheel with sweaty palms. She hated driving in San Francisco, which was why she took public transportation. It rarely ran on time, and she didn't want to be late picking up the kids, so she'd driven Fallon's car this morning. If only being on the road was the reason for the case of nerves.

A talk show host's voice droned on the radio. Hadley repositioned her hands. She focused on the traffic, ignoring the man in the passenger seat.

"You okay?" Blaise asked.

"Fine." Hadley didn't glance his way. She couldn't allow herself to be distracted and get in an accident.

"I thought Portland traffic was bad, but I forgot

how congested The City is," he said.

"I prefer taking Muni. I don't have to deal with traffic or parking."

No longer tapping on his cell phone, he angled his shoulders in her direction. Well, as much as the seat belt across his chest allowed. "Why are you driving today?"

A woodsy, pine scent kept tickling her nose. "The kids."

"No school bus?"

She couldn't tell if the fragrance was his soap or aftershave, but he smelled good, and she forced herself not to take another sniff. "There is, but someone needs to be home when they arrive."

Potential client, she reminded herself. Emphasis on *potential*.

Some people might be flattered that Blaise Mortenson had dropped everything and flown to meet her.

Not Hadley.

The man was trouble with a capital T. Not only because of his money and influence with the clientele who kept her in business. But also because he was a tasty piece of eye candy.

Blaise's photographs hadn't done him justice.

His dark chocolate eyes were a shade lighter than his thick hair and neatly trimmed beard. The combination—gorgeous. Wearing a tailored suit and leather shoes, he was the definition of a hottie. Well, if you went for the handsome-as-sin billionaire business type.

"You mentioned your niece and nephew are young," he said.

"Six and seven." She turned on her blinker before merging right. "They attend an after-school program if no one is home, but with their mother out of town, I wanted to pick them up on time today. I won't be able to the rest of the week."

"You're that busy?"

She nearly laughed at his surprise. Although she got that a lot.

"I am." Hadley shot him a sideward glance. "Did you think I was kidding when I said my next opening was in December?"

He half laughed. "Yes."

"Matchmaking and dating services are big business both in the US and abroad."

If she took him on as a client—and that was a big if—Hadley was curious about the specific traits he wanted in a wife. Patience and independence were usually high on the list with her elite clientele because of the hours they worked. Intelligence came next—especially for those in tech. Many looked for a partner who was accomplished in a chosen field. Intelligence often gave candidates an edge.

He glanced over his left shoulder. "Lex is still with us."

She glanced in the rearview mirror to see the

massive black SUV following her. Hard to believe she had the cell number of a professional bodyguard in her contacts now, but Lex had wanted her number as a precaution. For what, she didn't know, and honestly, didn't want to know.

"You could have ridden with him."

Blaise shrugged. "It'll give Lex a chance to see if the tracker works."

Her gaze jerked to Blaise before she stared at the street again. "Tracker? Internal or…"

"External," he said. "A friend built a prototype for a security application."

"You're a beta tester."

Blaise nodded. "My friend is likely the only one excited about my sudden trip to San Francisco. Or will be once he finds out. Present company included."

Hadley didn't need Blaise to tell her he'd rather be at his office. Each flash of annoyance when he glanced at another email or text on his phone told her that.

Her palms sweated more. "Let's hope you don't have to test whether or not the tracker works."

"The bodyguard and the prototype are precautions because of something that recently happened. It's no big deal," he said, nonchalantly. "Only a handful of people know where I am at the moment. But even if more did, I'd be fine on my own here."

"Confident."

"Yes, but not reckless. I do what's required of me."

Several of her clients had security teams. Some bodyguards had come into her office rather than staying in the lobby as Lex had.

"Do you ever worry?" she asked.

"About?"

"Kidnappers, attacks, false accusations, frivolous lawsuits, gold-diggers?"

He laughed. "That's quite a list."

It was her turn to shrug.

"It's part of the package. Lifestyle, so to speak," he admitted. "Having money comes with its own challenges. Security depends on how well-known you are and how many people you've upset along the way, but I prefer dealing with all this to…"

"What?"

"Not being wealthy."

She pulled behind a white Mercedes that was in the line of cars waiting to pick up students.

He peered out the window. "What is everyone waiting for?"

"Their kids. This is the pickup line. The students are brought out after the final bell."

"It's orderly."

"You don't want to be the person who goes against the flow. There is a procedure that must be followed."

"Sounds like your kind of place."

Okay, that was funny. Hadley hadn't known whether or not he had a sense of humor. She grinned. "It is."

Maybe this afternoon wouldn't be horrible. Hadley wasn't sure why she'd agreed to have Blaise tag along with her. Perhaps it was his ignorance over what an afternoon with two active children would be like. This would be a lesson for him and also a way to see how he responded to the unexpected because he would be in for a surprise.

"You mentioned the kids' mom," he said.

"She's my younger sister. They live with me."

"What about their dad?"

The innocent questions made Hadley's muscles tense. What happened to Clint wasn't a secret. The media had covered his arrest and trial for months. But her heart hurt for Fallon and what the guy had put her and the kids through.

"They're divorced. He's in jail." Hadley hated saying the name of the company so she whispered it.

He gasped. Not surprising since the scandal had extended far beyond the Financial District in San Francisco.

"That had to be rough," Blaise said, compassion in his voice.

"It was. My sister wasn't involved, but they questioned her as if she were. I'm not sure I know all of what my sister went through."

But Hadley hoped someday Fallon would tell her

everything. Until then, she wouldn't push.

"I'm sorry that happened to your sister, but she's fortunate to have you in her corner."

"Always." The same way Fallon was in hers. Maybe Hadley could use this as an opening to learn more about him. She'd searched his name after their phone call and was surprised to see little online about his personal life. "Do you have any brothers and sisters?"

Blaise's face hardened. "I'm an only child."

"Are your parents in the Portland area?"

"No." The word came out hard. "What about yours?"

"Retired and living their best lives on a cruise ship." Her mom and dad had worked and saved for years. They'd taught her from a young age to go after what she wanted, and she had. The same as they did with their retirement. "We see them a few times a year, but we talk weekly. They left San Francisco before Fallon's life fell apart."

"What grades are her kids in?"

Interesting. Blaise had flipped the conversation back to her. "First and second."

"Good kids?"

"The best." Hadley hadn't believed it was possible to love two children that much. "But I'm their aunt so I'm biased."

She drove forward to see the two kids waiting in line for her. As both waved, her heart filled with warmth. She'd never had time for pets or plants. Building her business had been the priority, but now...

"Are your niece and nephew the ones waving?" Blaise asked.

"Yes." Seeing the two kids' smiling faces brightened her day.

Thanks to Fallon and her children, Hadley had learned how much she'd been missing out on by spending all her time working. She enjoyed watching Audra and Ryder grow taller, noticing the changes in their faces, and hearing their new vocabulary.

A volunteer from the school helped the kids into the car. They scrambled into their seats and buckled in.

"Tug on your belts, please," Hadley said as if they were passengers on a theme park ride.

Ryder did and then leaned forward slightly. "Guess what happened today, Aunt Hadley?"

His excitement level suggested it was something big. "What?"

"Chloe Gold had a bloody nose at recess." He made a face. "It was so gross."

"No one hit her," Audra explained in her seven-going-on-seventeen tone.

"She has infected sinuses," Ryder added.

Audra snorted. "A sinus infection, silly."

"I'm not silly."

"Then you're stupid," Audra shot back.

Hadley cringed. "Kids…"

"Am not!" Ryder yelled.

"Are too."

Hadley cleared her throat and then pulled over to the side of the road. No way could she drive and talk to them at the same time the way Fallon did.

"Aunt Hadley." Audra sounded scandalized. "You're blocking someone's driveway. You'll get in trouble. They might arrest you."

"We won't be here long enough to get in trouble." Hadley shifted positions so she could see the kids, who were sending dagger-filled glances at each other. "If the police come, I'll explain why I had to stop."

Both kids' faces paled and guilty expressions formed. Ryder's bottom lip stuck out in a huge pout.

Hadley's gaze bounced between them. "Your mother doesn't allow you to use the word stupid."

A smug expression spread across Ryder's face. "Audra said it, not me."

"Your mom also doesn't like when you and your sister fight," Hadley added in case Ryder thought he was an innocent party. Disagreeing was one thing, but name-calling was a big no-no. The kids knew this.

Audra sighed. "I'm sorry for saying that, Aunt Hadley, and whoever else is in the front seat."

Blaise appeared to be trying not to laugh. She enjoyed seeing him relaxed, though she wished it was under better circumstances. "I'm texting Lex to make sure he knows everything is okay."

"Thanks."

The bodyguard storming up to the car would frighten the kids. Months after Clint's arrest, sirens continued to scare Ryder and flashing lights upset Audra. No doubt she mentioned the police because of what happened to their dad.

And to them.

"Who's Lex?" Audra asked, ever curious.

"Let's stay on-topic." Hadley kept her gaze on her niece. "You apologized but not to the person you offended. What are you going to do about that?"

As Audra's narrow shoulders sagged, her mouth twisted. She stared at her brother. "I'm sorry, Ryder. You're not stupid."

Ryder nodded once. "I'm not, and I forgive you."

That didn't take long. Hadley noticed the black SUV through the hatchback window.

"Lex stopped behind us if you want to catch a ride with him," Hadley said to Blaise, repositioning herself in the driver's seat. She wanted to give him an out from the kids now that he'd gotten a taste of them and their squabble. The afternoon would go downhill from here as the witching hour—what Fallon called the late afternoon and early evening—grew closer.

"No need," he replied.

She put the car in gear, turned on the blinker, and merged onto the street. "Kids, I want you to meet Mr. Mortenson. He's spending the afternoon with us.

Please introduce yourselves."

"I'm Audra Caples." Her voice didn't waver. "Does your beard itch?"

Blaise rubbed his fingers over his facial hair. "Not now, but it did when I was first growing it."

"I want to have a beard," Ryder chimed in. "I'm Ryder. I'm Audra's brother. Are you Aunt Hadley's boyfriend?"

"No," she and Blaise said at the same time.

"Mr. Mortenson is considering working with me," Hadley clarified.

"Oh," Audra said knowingly. "You're going to find him a wife."

"Possibly." Hadley saw the humor in his gaze. He appeared amused, but that might change after hours with the kids. "That's why we're going to talk."

"Since we have a guest, can we go for ice cream after Ryder's soccer game?" Audra asked.

Hadley should have seen that one coming. "We'll see. You have dance class first."

"Aunt Hadley didn't say no so that means we get ice cream, Mr. Mortenson," Audra explained.

Hadley glanced at her niece for a moment. "No, it doesn't."

"It has every single other time," Audra said.

"Good for you on recognizing a pattern. That's an excellent skill," Blaise said. "And I appreciate you sharing insights about your aunt."

Sure, he did. Only because the info might help

him.

He should, however, know one thing about her. "I'm an open book. What you see is what you get."

"No secrets that need to be pried out of you?"

"Not really." Oh, she had them, but none that she wanted to tell anyone. Especially him.

* * *

The temperature was in the mid-seventies for Ryder's game. Blaise stood on the sidelines without his suit jacket, which was in Hadley's car, feeling as if he had stepped into an alternative universe.

Little kids, similar in size to Ryder, stumbled and ran on the makeshift field. Chasing the ball seemed a more apt description than passing it. Orange cones marked the sidelines with two collapsible nets on either side.

This appeared to be one step up from daycare, given the chaos. At least he was outdoors and not stuck inside the dance studio lobby with parents and siblings who didn't understand the concept of talking quietly.

Hadley stood next to Blaise. Audra sat on her left.

He didn't know what to make of the matchmaker. Hadley had gone from hard-nosed outside her office to doting aunt the minute the kids appeared. Though she hadn't let them get away with much in the car or during their ten-minute stop at home to change clothes and grab a snack—string cheese, apple slices, and Goldfish crackers.

He'd thought she was joking about not having any free time to speak with him. Now he wasn't so sure.

Blaise loosened his tie. He had a feeling they would be here a while.

A boy kicked a goal. His team cheered. So did people standing near them. "Aren't there teams? Sides?"

"They don't keep score at this age," Hadley explained.

"Of course, they do." Blaise stared at her in disbelief. "The kids keep score in their heads."

"This is for fun and to learn skills."

She sounded serious as if she bought into the no scores and everyone gets a participation medal. He wouldn't have expected that. "Kids still want to win."

"They're only six. Kids enjoy making goals."

"To score."

She shook her head.

Blaise nearly laughed. Jocks and geeks alike wanted to be on the winning team. He would prove it to Hadley, and he knew just the person to help him.

He walked around Hadley to where her niece sat playing a game on a tablet. "Hey, Audra."

She glanced up. "Yes, Mr. M?"

Audra and Ryder had started calling Blaise that after her dance lesson. Maybe Mortenson was too long of a name for them to say.

"What's your favorite thing when you play a game with your brother or friends?" he asked.

"Beating everybody." She grinned, a tooth missing from her smile. "I like to win."

He held up his hand to the girl. "Give me a high five."

She did.

Satisfaction flowing through him, Blaise glanced over at Hadley. "See?"

"That's one data point."

He noticed the moms, dads, maybe a few grandparents given the gray hair, watching the soccer game. "I can find more."

"That's okay." Hadley clapped when Ryder entered the game. "I'll ask my sister when she calls tonight."

"Will you admit defeat if I'm correct?"

Hadley blew out a breath. "This isn't a battle, but I'll tell you what she says."

He hoped that meant she would let him hire her.

"Sit next to me, Mr. M." Audra patted the empty folding chair on her left. "My aunt always stands."

"Better view this way." As Hadley grinned at Ryder on the field, her face lit up.

Blaise's breath stilled. He found himself mesmerized.

"Go sit," she added. "You've had a long day. You must be tired."

Not tired. More wanting to finish his business and get home because this day hadn't turned out as he planned. "Thanks."

On the field, a boy with blond curls picked a dandelion. Okay, maybe that was the one kid who didn't care about winning. But the grin on his face suggested he was having as much fun as his teammates at the opposite goal.

Blaise glanced at his phone. Five past five. Time was ticking, and he wanted to make an earlier flight.

He leaned toward Audra to whisper in her ear. "How long is the game?"

"Too long." She shook her head. "They still have to have halftime."

Halftime? He perked up. "How long does that last?"

Audra shrugged.

"Not long enough for our meeting if that's what you want to know." Hadley's gaze pinned him.

He held up his hands. "I only asked a question. Pee wee soccer isn't my usual venue."

"Fine, but it's not too late to have Lex take you to your hotel and we can meet in the morning."

"I don't mind if you have the meeting now," Audra said with a thoughtful expression on her face.

"Thanks, sweetie." Hadley touched the girl's shoulder. "But I want to watch Ryder. I told Mr. Mortenson the two of you come before our meeting."

The girl straightened. "If you marry him, you

won't have to have a meeting."

Whoa. The kid had it all wrong.

"I can't date a client," Hadley said before Blaise could respond.

That was a good rule. Not that he wanted to hire Hadley's services for himself, but he needed to explain the situation in person. Which he'd hoped to do already.

The corners of Audra's mouth turned down. "But Ryder and I need an uncle. Colby has an uncle who plays four-square with him. Mr. M could do that with us and other stuff."

No, Blaise couldn't.

Nothing against the kid. She appeared to be potty-trained and able to speak in full sentences. She also hadn't vomited yet. All plusses, or maybe that was normal for seven-year-olds.

Or was she six? He couldn't remember.

"Colby's dad died." Audra's voice was softer than it had been. "Ours is still alive, but it feels like he's dead. Even before he went to jail, he wasn't around."

Blaise sat, unable to speak. Not from what the girl had said, but from understanding the emotion behind her words. He'd been part of a happy family, but drugs had stolen his parents from him. Once that happened, his mom and dad hadn't been around because they'd either been high or chasing the next fix.

Hadley kneeled next to Audra's chair. "It's hard

not having your dad around, but he loves you. Your parents aren't together now, but that doesn't change how they feel about you and Ryder."

Audra nodded. "That's what Mom says."

Blaise remembered what Hadley had told him about her sister.

They're divorced. He's in jail.

Caples.

The kids' last name sounded so familiar.

And then it hit him.

Hadley had told him the name of the firm, but he finally connected the dots. Their dad must be Clint Caples. He and three others had nearly taken down an investment firm with their shady dealings. The scandal had riveted the finance world.

"Wait…" Eyes wide, Audra glanced up at Blaise. "If you can't marry Aunt Hadley, you can marry my mom. She's pretty. And nice. Except when you want an extra cookie. Or forget to clean your room, then she gets on you. But if you put your dirty clothes in the hamper, I'm sure you'll get along fine."

Oh, boy. Blaise had no idea what to say. He rubbed his neck.

"That won't work because Mr. Mortenson doesn't live in San Francisco," Hadley said as if that was the only reason against the marriage. "He's only in town for a meeting and will fly home to Oregon tomorrow."

"Tonight," Blaise said a beat after her.

"You should stay," Audra said in a matter-of-fact tone. "Aunt Hadley makes lasagna for dinner on Tuesdays. It's my favorite. Though Ryder likes her enchilada pie better."

"Sorry I'll miss it."

"Maybe when you come back," Audra said as if she believed this was only the first time she would see him.

His next trip to San Francisco wouldn't be to visit Hadley. He doubted he would see Audra or her brother after tonight. Still, Blaise nodded.

"Ryder has the ball," Hadley said, sounding excited.

The boy ran toward the goal with the others chasing after him. He kicked and scored.

Hadley and Audra cheered. People clapped. The coach gave Ryder a high five. The boy's face lit up.

Blaise's breath caught. He was glad Ryder had this team and a coach. One person could make all the difference to a kid. His high school math teacher had gone above and beyond for Blaise. So had the school's custodian.

Both had initially reported Blaise's home situation to a school administrator. He'd resented them for doing that until he learned filing a report was mandatory because of their jobs. In doing so, they'd fulfilled their obligation and then could help him.

His eyes stung. He rubbed whatever it was irritating them. Must be pollen or something in the air.

"Do you play soccer, Mr. M?" Audra asked.

"I did when I was in school. During PE class."

Her eyebrows drew together. "You weren't on a team after school, too?"

"No."

"That's too bad."

The familiar ache—a small one that was always present—grew larger. He ignored it. The same way he tried to put his past behind him. This wasn't the time to explain to a kid, however bright she might be, about his junkie parents. All he could do was nod.

Her gaze narrowed. "Do you like soccer?"

"I like it a lot."

Audra rubbed her chin. "You should join a team now. They have ones for old people."

Out of the mouth of babes. He laughed.

Hadley gasped. "Mr. Mortenson isn't old. He's younger than me."

Interesting. She must have researched him. Even if he was younger, it couldn't be by much. A year or two at most. "Everyone is old when you're seven."

Audra nodded so he must have guessed her age correctly. "See, Aunt Hadley?"

"You need a lesson in manners." Hadley sounded more amused than angry. She looked at him. "Go to the car, if you need to work."

Lex was around so Blaise could sit in the SUV, too. His cell phone had been relatively quiet.

Whatever was in his inbox could wait for now. "Maybe at halftime."

Ryder kicked the ball away from an opponent. Blaise clapped. "Way to go, Ryder."

The kid grinned at Blaise before giving the thumbs-up sign. Blaise returned the gesture.

He didn't care about the game—there were a hundred other places he would rather be—but he didn't want to desert the kids. He'd been there, and it sucked. Ryder and Audra had been through enough at their young ages. Even though they were strangers, the least Blaise could do was stay here and cheer.

And he did.

Chapter Five

Somehow Hadley survived the afternoon and evening. Standing at the sink, she rinsed off a plate. Blaise, however, appeared ready for a nap—or bedtime with the way he yawned. She would have thought a CEO would have more energy. Though, kids could be draining in a different way than leading a team of employees or attending meetings.

As she finished doing the dishes, he sat at the table with Audra and Ryder. The kids filled in math worksheets while he worked on his laptop. The only one who seemed unhappy with their guest was the cat. Tiny had disappeared after they arrived home. Most likely he was under a bed.

Blaise glanced from the computer to the kids' worksheet. Concern filled his gaze.

Talk about adorable.

He must have noticed a mistake because he reached his hand toward Ryder's paper before pulling it away.

Blaise bit his lip.

Poor guy, he didn't know what to say or do.

He'd suffered enough through the dance class, soccer game, ice cream shop, and dinner. He'd even removed his shoes like the kids had when they arrived home.

The least she could do was help him out. "Did you both check your work?"

Audra nodded.

"Oops." Ryder raised his pencil. Suddenly, his eyes widened, and he erased something.

Blaise's relief was palpable.

She faced the sink to keep from laughing.

After Hadley loaded the last plate into the dishwasher, she glanced at the microwave clock. "Okay, kids. It's time to get ready for bed."

Blaise perked up. "Does this mean it's almost time?"

"To read a story?" she teased.

"Ha ha."

Too bad she wasn't joking, but he'd been better with the kids than she thought he would be. He hadn't been silent after he sent Lex to a hotel to rest and wait for his call. Blaise had even eaten two servings of the crockpot turkey chili.

"You laugh now," she joked. "But just you wait and see."

He glanced at the time. "After story time?"

She nodded. "We can talk business."

A brilliant smile crinkled the corners of his eyes and took her breath away. No man should look that hot. At least, finding him a wife wouldn't be that difficult. He checked all the boxes.

✓ Gorgeous
✓ Nice
✓ Smart
✓ Rich

She never made the final decision about taking on a client until talking to the person and making sure what they wanted aligned with the service she provided. So far, though, she had no reason not to want to work with Blaise. And yes, spending the additional time with him was helping her feel that way.

The arrogance he'd displayed during their phone call wasn't something new to her. That level of cockiness often went with the job title and net worth. Yet, she appreciated the way he'd toned it down in front of the kids. Well, other than at the soccer game about keeping score, but Audra had been too busy playing the game on her tablet to pay attention to what they were discussing.

He dressed well, but Hadley didn't know if he chose his own clothes or hired someone to shop for him. Either way, the style worked for him. Some clients needed fashion makeovers before dating because a wardrobe needed more than shorts, sweats, jeans, graphic T-shirts, and hoodies.

"Finished," Audra said.

"Me, too." Ryder placed his pencil on the table. "You know what that means."

Both kids scrambled from the table and ran toward their bedroom.

Blaise stared after them. "Where are they going?"

"To get ready for bed."

"So we can—"

"After their bedtime routine."

She waited for him to ask how long that would take, but he went back to work on his computer, so she made the kids lunches for tomorrow.

Twenty minutes later, Audra appeared wearing her favorite pajamas, the ones covered in cute llamas. "Ryder is getting out of the shower."

That was Hadley's signal; the kids were almost ready for her. "Teeth brushed?"

Audra showed off her pearly whites. "Clean and minty fresh."

"Good job." Hadley dried her hands on a kitchen towel. "Let's go."

"Ryder wants Blaise to read to us tonight," Audra said. "I don't mind if he does."

Her hopeful tone suggested she wanted that, too.

Hadley glanced at Blaise. "That's usually my job, but you're welcome to it."

Audra bounced on the tips of her toes but didn't speak.

He hesitated, a wary gleam in his eyes. "I haven't read a story to someone, most likely myself, in a couple of decades."

"This will be a much easier audience to please than investors," Hadley encouraged.

He closed his laptop and stood. "Lead the way."

Audra did.

Hadley added soap and then turned on the dishwasher. By the time she reached the kids' room, Blaise was sitting on the edge of Ryder's bed and reading from C.S. Lewis's *The Lion, The Witch and The Wardrobe*. As if entranced, the kids stared at him.

Seeing her niece and nephew enthralled didn't surprise Hadley, but the book wasn't the one they'd been reading last night. And then she remembered— after Clint's sentencing, a box addressed to the kids had arrived from Cassandra's Attic. Inside had been *The Chronicles of Narnia* in paperback but no note. The kids were certain their dad had sent it, but Clint had never said a word about the books.

Blaise closed the cover. "That's a chapter for each of you."

"Thank you, Mr. M." Audra cuddled her stuffed llama. "You did good."

Ryder held on to a shark. His space-ship-themed pajamas didn't coordinate with his stuffed animal. "Really good."

"Thank you," Blaise said. "So…"

"You need to check for monsters. Under here first." Audra pointed to the bottom of the beds and at the closet. "Over there."

"Is that where they hide?" he asked.

Audra nodded. "Either my mom or aunt checks every night."

"Sometimes both of them," Ryder added. "That way we're safe. Nothing will come out and scare us in the middle of the night."

Hadley held her breath, praying Blaise wouldn't laugh at the kids. They'd had nightmares for months after Clint's arrest in front of them. They'd watched investigators carry out computers, electronics, and other items from the only home they'd ever known, one that no longer belonged to them.

"We can't have anyone getting scared." Blaise kneeled between the two beds. He checked under Audra's and then Ryder's, sticking his arm underneath. "These are clear of monsters except for one cat who is giving me the evil eye."

"That's Tiny," Audra explained. "Only he's big now."

"Big and fat and sleeps all the time," Ryder added. "Now the closet."

As Blaise turned, he caught Hadley's eye and

smiled. "We're making sure no monsters are hiding."

"You look as if you have experience doing this."

He winked, sending her pulse stuttering. "I'm a fast learner."

Blaise opened the door, pushed the clothes aside, and stepped inside, which was something neither she nor Fallon had ever done. After he stepped out and closed the door, he focused on the kids. "All clear. No monsters in there, either."

The kids cheered.

"Is there anything else you need?" he asked them.

"You need to tuck us in," Audra said.

His forehead creased. "You're already in bed."

"Yes, but we're not tucked in," Ryder explained.

Blaise's glance went from one child to the other. "I don't know what that means."

Audra's eyes widened. "Didn't your parents tuck you in?"

"No." His voice was hoarse. He cleared his throat. "My parents never did that."

Or if they had, he didn't remember, Hadley thought.

Blaise's sad tone tugged at her heart. She went toward the bed.

"Can you two teach me how to do it?" he asked the kids.

Hadley stopped.

"Sure," Audra said. "You take the edges of the sheet and blanket and tuck them under the mattress."

"Nice and tight so we don't fall out," Ryder added.

Blaise did as instructed to both. "How did I do?"

"Great," Audra announced.

Ryder nodded. "The bestest. Thanks."

Blaise shifted his weight between his feet. "Goodnight?"

He almost appeared nervous, which endeared him to Hadley more.

"Okay, you guys. Lights out." She kissed each child on their forehead before turning off the light on the nightstand between the two beds. "I love you both. Sweet dreams."

Blaise followed her into the living room where he sat on the couch. "Now is it time for our meeting?"

"Yes, I just—"

Her phone rang in the kitchen. "It's probably my sister. She'll want an update on the kids. I'll make it fast."

Another ring sounded.

Blaise yawned. "I've waited this long. Another five minutes doesn't matter."

She hurried and grabbed her phone from the counter. Fallon's name and number appeared on the screen.

Hadley answered. "How's LA?"

"Not bad, but I miss everyone. How did today go?"

"Well." She gave a brief rundown of everything

including the soccer game. "By the way, do you think Ryder knows the score even though there's no scoreboard?"

"He's told me the score after a game, so yes. I keep track, too, though I've never mentioned it to him."

Guess Blaise was right.

"Competition is part of human nature," Fallon added. "Then again, I was more into sports than you were."

"You still are." Hadley glanced at the time. "The kids are in bed, and I have a meeting."

"At this hour?"

"Long story, which I'll tell you when you get home." Otherwise, she would keep Blaise waiting. Again. "Talk to you tomorrow."

Hadley plugged in her phone to charge and went into the living room. "That was..."

Blaise was asleep on the couch, his head resting against a throw pillow. The corners of his mouth tipped upward. He looked so peaceful and young. Nothing like the businessman who'd wanted an appointment with her this afternoon.

"Blaise?" she asked.

He didn't stir.

The day must have caught up with him, but should she let Blaise sleep?

Hadley knew someone who might tell her. She went into the kitchen for her phone and typed a text.

Hadley: *Blaise fell asleep on my couch. Should I wake him?*
Lex (Bodyguard): *Let him sleep. Have him call me in the morning.*
Hadley: *Will do.*
Lex (Bodyguard): *He'll want coffee as soon as he wakes up.*
Hadley: *Thanks for letting me know.*

After double-checking that her phone was charging, Hadley grabbed the fleece blanket from a nearby chair and covered Blaise with it. She couldn't tuck in the edges, but this would keep him warm enough. He wouldn't care about monsters which meant the only thing else missing from the bedtime routine was a kiss on the forehead.

But she didn't dare.

Instead, she allowed her gaze to linger on his handsome face. "Sweet dreams, Blaise."

Hadley had a feeling when he woke up, his serene expression would be nothing more than a memory.

* * *

Sunlight streamed onto his face. That was odd because Blaise usually woke when it was dark outside. He also hadn't heard his alarm beep.

What was going on?

Staring at the ceiling, his dry eyes burned. He blinked. And then he realized...

84

I slept in my contacts.

How had that happened?

And why was his neck achy? His back was stiff, too. At least no headache. Except something was on top of him.

Something heavy.

Two wide green eyes met his. The cat, not-so-tiny Tiny, was lying on his chest.

"Good morning?" Blaise wasn't sure what to say to a cat. He'd never had pets growing up. He wasn't home enough to have one now. "You have too much padding to be hungry."

White whiskers twitched.

"I need to get up, so please move."

The cat remained where he was and continued to stare at him.

Okay, Blaise was bigger. He could handle Tiny.

Outside, what sounded like a garbage truck drove past.

The cat jumped off of him.

"You need a new name, Tiny." Blaise sat up.

A plaid fleece blanket fell to his waist. He didn't remember covering himself with it, which meant someone else—most likely Hadley—had. His suit jacket hung off the back of a green velvet chair. Two backpacks sat near his computer bag on the floor. Shoes, too.

He'd been on the couch and closed his eyes for a few minutes. He must have fallen sound asleep. The consequences of doing that hit hard. He not only had missed his chance to speak with Hadley but also to return home last night. The day must have worn him out, which was unusual. He hadn't had time for more nano-naps. Maybe those worked better than he imagined.

Blaise dragged his hand through his hair and then stretched his arms over his head. He needed to take out his contacts, shower, and brush his teeth. His bag with a change of clothes was with Lex. Who was probably wondering where he was.

He reached for his phone, but it wasn't in his pocket. Panic shot through him. He had no idea of the time. The markets could be open by now.

"You're awake." Hadley stood in the entrance to the living room. Holding a wooden spoon, she wore a pink apron covered in red hearts over her white shirt and black pants.

His heart beat faster. Something that had nothing to do with his being out of touch with the rest of the world.

Weird.

Because he didn't understand the reaction.

Yes, Hadley was pretty, but seeing her now flipped his stomach inside out. He hadn't felt this way in years. Back then, work had triggered the reaction. A woman never had. He must be tired.

Blaise rolled his head to one side, stretching the muscles in his neck. "I'm sorry I fell asleep."

"No apology needed," she said. "Kids wear you out whether or not you're used to it."

"Our meeting…"

"Will happen this morning."

Hadley didn't have to tell him her priority was getting the kids to school. "At nine," he confirmed.

She nodded.

Just as she'd told him yesterday. Blaise half laughed. "Proud of yourself for being right?"

Hadley shrugged. "Not really, because you wanted to get home last night."

He hadn't expected her to acknowledge that. "I need to text Lex."

"I did after you fell asleep. When you're ready to leave, let him know. Your phone is charging in the kitchen."

That was thoughtful of her, but after seeing Hadley Lowell in action, he had a feeling she wasn't as rigid as he first imagined. "Thanks."

"My sister called last night. You were correct about the game scores. Fallon said she and Ryder keep track."

The victory was hollow because he was in San Francisco when he should be in his own bed in Portland. "Now you know."

Hadley studied him like he was a lab rat. "I thought you'd rub it in."

"You didn't rub in me falling asleep and missing our chance to talk. Why would I do that to you?"

"Bad assumption."

Not really, because in another instance he may have. He stood. "I'm going to use the bathroom."

"Washcloths are under the sink. New toothbrushes are in the second drawer."

Curiosity got the better of him. "Do you keep a supply for overnight guests?"

"Audra and Ryder's friends sometimes forget to bring things when they stay over, and toothbrushes are the number one item."

So she hadn't meant adult overnight guests. That was good. Not that he cared. What she did was none of his business. Still, he wondered. She didn't go out with clients, but an attractive, successful woman must date. Did she have a boyfriend? Or a special guy she spent time with?

"Not that we have a ton of space for sleepovers, but we make do."

He glanced around. "Your condo is nice."

She smiled. "I love it, but I bought this when it was only me. I need to find a bigger place for us."

Us meaning Hadley, her sister, the kids, and the cat. "Have you started looking?"

"Yes, but I want to stay in this neighborhood so it'll take time."

If she wanted something bigger, he didn't understand why she wouldn't just buy a new house and move. "Lack of inventory around here?"

"Money." She toyed with the edge of her apron.

"Houses are pricier than condos."

"Oh, right." Which he should know. Except he'd buried what being poor was like. Well, tried. The bad memories outweighed the good ones by a hundred to one so why hold on to them?

"It'll happen," she said.

"You have a plan."

Hadley laughed. "I do."

And now Blaise had one, too. Everyone had a price. He'd said that to Trevor. Unknowingly, Hadley had told Blaise hers—a house for her family. An expensive one. He could make that happen for her. Today, tomorrow, whenever she wanted.

He forced himself not to grin too widely.

"A fresh pot of coffee is brewing," she said. "There's a clean mug sitting on the counter."

"Are you making breakfast?"

"Dinner. The crock pot comes in handy with work and kids."

"I've never used one." He had no idea if he owned a slow cooker. Someone else had set up his kitchen when he moved in. His housekeeper, Robyn, did his shopping. He also had a personal chef.

"We use ours too much, but it saves time." She wiped her hands on the front of her apron. "Today is pancakes and pajama day so the kids eat at school."

"Shouldn't take them long to get ready then. Crawl out of bed, brush teeth and hair, and go."

She shivered. "The kids can't wear the same

pajamas they wore overnight."

"All they did was sleep in them."

"For hours. They need clean ones."

That rigid side of her was showing again. "You're making more work for yourself."

"I don't mind. If you want cereal or I may have yogurt…"

"No, thanks." He didn't want her to go to any trouble for him. "All I need is a cup of coffee."

"Okay, I have to get the kids up."

She didn't give him a chance to respond before she walked away.

Maybe she wasn't a morning person. Maybe she hadn't had a cup of coffee yet. Or maybe she *was* as inflexible as he first believed, not only about work but also about life.

Still she cared about her work and her family. Her sister, niece, and nephew were lucky to have someone like Hadley. Other than a handful of friends, no one cared about Blaise. Not that way. The only people who did things for him were on his payroll. If things worked out as he planned during their meeting, Hadley would work for him, too.

And then she could buy whatever house she wanted.

Chapter Six

Later that morning, Hadley sat at her desk. Even though tempted, she hadn't poured herself a cup of coffee from the pot she'd made for Blaise and passed by the machine in the lobby. Whether Hadley remained awake all day, however, remained to be seen because she hadn't slept well last night. But that had more to do with Blaise sleeping in her living room than her going cold turkey.

Still, she was proud she'd survived another morning without a jolt of caffeine to get her going. She'd also checked off every item on her morning to-do list at home and at the office.

Next on her schedule—the nine o'clock meeting with Blaise.

Warmth spread through her veins.

Twenty-four hours ago, she'd never met him. She wouldn't call them friends, but she'd enjoyed spending time with him yesterday. He'd piqued her curiosity. She wanted to hear what he was looking for—a date, a girlfriend, a wife. A part of her envied whoever he ended up with because he was a catch.

And not only because of his net worth.

In some ways, Blaise was exactly the man she imagined he would be. Pushy, all business, not wanting to take no for an answer. But seeing him with Audra and Ryder had given Hadley a glimpse of a softer side. That appealed to her deep inside, a place she hadn't realized existed. Maybe that explained why he'd been on her mind since Lex picked him up at her condo two hours ago.

More than once, Blaise's confidence had wavered with the kids. The hint of vulnerability made him seem more approachable. The switch from standoffish to kind in a blink of an eye took his hotness to a new level.

She also had a feeling her niece and nephew would talk about Mr. M for days.

A part of her was crushing on him.

Harmless, yes, but she needed to focus on business. On his wanting to hire her. Anything else would only get in the way, especially if he became a client.

Ella poked her head into the office. "The receptionist from the front desk called. Blaise is on his way back."

"Thanks." Hadley glanced at the time on her screen.

8:59 AM.

Punctual. That was a good sign.

The outer door opened and closed.

Hadley rubbed her palms over her pants, took a breath, and then exhaled slowly.

"Hello, again." Blaise strode into her office with purposeful steps, his laptop bag in his left hand, and a dazzling smile on his face. He'd changed clothes. His yellow shirt and gray pants weren't as fancy as his suit yesterday, but the style looked good on him. He'd tamed the hair that had been a mess when he'd woken up, and he wore black glasses.

Flutters filled her stomach.

She swallowed.

Standing on the opposite side of her desk, he held out his right arm.

Hadley stood and shook his hand.

Tingles erupted at the point of contact. The feeling was unexpected. Not unenjoyable.

His skin was warm. His hand large.

And this was lasting far too long.

Crushing was one thing. Touching him? Avoid at all costs.

She pulled away, not understanding why his touch affected her, and motioned to the empty chair. "Please have a seat."

He did.

She was thankful the desk was between them. That was enough distance where she couldn't smell him—his aftershave or soap—like she could yesterday in the car.

Ella brought in coffee for him and left without saying a word.

Blaise raised the cup. "So here we are. At the time you said. So how do we start?"

"I like to begin by telling a little about myself."

"Go right ahead."

She rested her elbows on the desk and leaned forward. "I opened Matched by Lowell seven years ago after working for a few other matchmakers. My focus then, as it is now, is to find people their perfect match. Not only to date, though that's where everyone starts, but to connect two people whose journey together will lead them to a fulfilling life-long marriage. My services are rather old school with personal interviews and surveys. Which is why I limit who I accept as a client. I want to give each person the focus they deserve and have time to interview each person who might be a match. Any questions so far?"

He held his coffee cup. "No."

"The time we'd work together varies. There is no limit as to how long it takes to find a match. Some clients are with me for months. Others a year or two. One client took three years, but that is the exception not the norm. I can't guarantee a happily ever after, but I will do everything in my power to introduce you to people who can help you find one."

Blaise's smile was neon-lights-on-Broadway bright. "I read through the information you sent Trevor, but hearing you say this reaffirms we're on the same page. Your fees for such an individualized service are fair."

"Excellent." She opened her notebook and readied her pen. "Let's talk timeframe. Do you have one or are you flexible?"

"Is by the end of the month too soon?"

He grinned, but she couldn't tell if he was serious or not. She hoped not.

"Joking," he said. "But I would like things to happen as quickly as possible."

Her insides twisted, but she wasn't sure why given the reason he wanted to hire her. "Love at first sight has happened with clients, but that's a rarity. The norm is much slower."

"That's fine. I can be patient while you work your magic."

"Love isn't something you conjure up. If it was, I'd be out of business," she admitted. "Though I will admit when I look at two people to gauge their compatibility, there's a gut instinct involved."

"Magic."

"Are you playing devil's advocate?"

He winked. "Maybe."

The temperature in the office rose. Or maybe it was her. "When did you decide you wanted a serious relationship?"

"I don't want one."

Her gaze jerked to his. "I beg your pardon?"

"I don't want a girlfriend or to get married. Not now, maybe not ever."

Her mouth gaped. She closed it. Considered his words. Scratched her head. "Then why are you here?"

Wasting your time and mine?

"I need you to find two wives." The serious glint in his eyes told her he wasn't joking.

Hadley started to speak but then stopped herself. She leaned back in her chair before trying again.

"I thought there was nothing anyone could say that would shock me. You have." The wealthy could be eccentric but this was on another level and illegal. "Polygamy is against the law."

Blaise laughed. The deep, rich sound floated through the air, smacking into her and curling her toes. A totally inappropriate response to a man wanting two wives but not marriage.

What was wrong with her? And him?

"Based on the disgust on your face, I should clarify my needs." He sounded as if this was amusing to him. "The women won't be my wives."

Say what? That didn't clarify anything. "Whose wives would they be?"

"My two closest friends."

"That's…unusual." She sounded exasperated, exactly how she felt. Something about Blaise left her unsettled and off-kilter. She didn't like the feeling and wanted it to end.

"Is it?" he asked. "Henry Davenport is a good friend of mine. He thought you'd be able to help me."

So that was how Blaise had found her. She took client confidentiality seriously, but Henry must have said something to him. "Your friend and I have a special arrangement."

"Did you date him?"

Hadley laughed. Henry had never seen her as anything more than someone he hired. Staff, if that. Otherwise, she would have received an invitation to one of his elaborate birthday celebrations. She hadn't. "No."

"Does that mean you're the brains behind his matchmaking?"

"Henry has his own skills for pairing couples, but our styles…complement each other."

"Excellent." Blaise leaned forward in his chair. "That means you know how to match people who aren't your clients."

She didn't know what he was getting at. At this point, she wasn't sure she wanted to know. "As I said, my arrangement with Henry is one of a kind."

"No reason you can't have two of those 'arrangements.'"

"True…" But she needed more information to

decide what to do. "Why do you want your friends to get married so badly you're willing to hire a matchmaker for them?"

"I want them to be happy," Blaise said without missing a beat.

That begged a question. "They aren't happy now?"

Blaise's lips folded in. "They could be happier."

He wasn't telling her the truth. "Do they know what you're planning?"

"Not exactly." He rubbed his chin. "It will be a surprise."

"You hiring a matchmaker...or them falling in love with their perfect matches?"

He sipped his coffee as if he wanted to delay his answer. Or think of one. "Both."

"Sending your friends on a vacation is a surprise." This still made no sense to her. "Hiring your friends a matchmaker they don't want would be a mistake."

His face fell for a moment, but then his smile returned. "It's not a mistake. They won't think so after meeting the love of their life."

He sounded convinced. She wasn't. "They must be close friends for you to go to so much trouble."

His eyes darted around the office. "They are."

He might believe that, but based on Blaise's body language, he was holding back information.

She tapped her finger against her chin. "What aren't you telling me?"

He crossed his leg over his knee. "What do you mean? I have two friends, and I want you to find them wives."

"Something isn't adding up. And if Henry's involved, there's more to the situation than what you've told me."

Blaise scratched his neck. "If you're worried, this is like his birthday adventure pairings, it isn't."

"Then what is it? Why do your friends need wives now?"

A beat passed. And another.

A sheepish expression crossed his face. "There's a bet."

I knew this went beyond friendship.

But she also realized Blaise Mortenson was as much trouble as she thought he would be. She steepled her fingers. "Go on."

"Five years ago, six of us made a bet. The last single man wins." A muscle ticked at his jawline. "We each contributed ten million dollars. We created a fund that my company runs and we agreed to use the money to test an investment algorithm I'd been developing. The return exceeded my expectations."

"How well did it do?"

"The fund is worth five hundred million dollars."

Her lips parted. That amount explained his motivation for wanting his friends to get married.

"Winner takes all, unless all of us marry within a year of the first person," he explained. "The first wedding occurred nine months ago. The third was on Saturday. That's when I decided I wanted to speed things up so I win sooner."

"By finding the other two wives," she offered.

"It's a brilliant idea."

Cockiness oozed from him. She shouldn't find that as attractive as she did. Usually that was a turn-off. "That remains to be seen."

But she had her doubts.

"My friends will have zero complaints once they meet the women of their dreams. Which is where you come in. I need to make sure they end up with the right women. Not gold-diggers or divas."

Hadley bit her lip, unsure of what she wanted to say next. "What you're asking goes beyond what I do for Henry."

"New skills are good to have."

"Not sure how marketable these would be."

"I'll give you my highest recommendation."

"Thanks, but you're single and not planning to settle down." Which was too bad. "Are your friends dating or are they trying to win the bet, too?"

"Neither is pursuing nor dating anyone. Both would be open to meeting someone. The bet doesn't seem important to them. One forgot about it. The other doesn't seem to care much about winning."

Blaise appeared to have justified his actions, but that didn't make his plan right. She studied him, trying to see beneath the gorgeous outer package. "But the bet is to you."

He nodded once.

Having the most money was a way for some wealthy clients to quantify their success with spots on a Richest in America list. Though a few shied away from that and didn't want to be listed or even known to the public. Which was Blaise?

"Do you want to win because of the money or something else?" she asked.

Blaise stared down his nose at her. "What I want doesn't affect you or anyone else. It's personal."

Touchy. He had to be hiding something. "Have your friends mentioned being interested in marriage?"

"No, but they are. Everyone is."

"You said you weren't."

"I was speaking literally. As in right now." He leaned back in the chair. "But I'm okay whether or not it happens. Marriage has never been a life goal. But my friends? They will be great husbands. This will be a win for all three of us."

She hesitated. "Maybe, but I have a bad feeling about this."

"You're cautious. A planner." Blaise didn't miss a beat responding. "That means you should be questioning the situation. And me."

"I'm past the point of questioning," she admitted. "My gut is telling me no."

He sat forward. "Why?"

"How many reasons do you want to hear?"

Blaise laughed. "Henry said you were thorough so I should have known there would be more than one. What's your biggest reason?"

"Finding matches without your friends' input and meeting them in person will be impossible."

"I know both well. We're close."

"As a friend, maybe. But you can't see inside their heads or peek into their hearts."

"I'm willing to take that risk," he countered.

"It's not your reputation at stake."

"One million dollars. Each."

"I don't understand."

"I'll pay you a million dollars for each of my friends if they marry a woman you pick out for them. If they both marry your matches, I'll give you a million-dollar bonus."

Three million dollars?

Shock poured through her. She may have gasped. Most people would with an offer like that. It was a dream-come-true amount. She could sell her condo and buy a house in the Marina District. Not next year or the year after that, but as soon as the money cleared in her bank account.

She placed her hand on her knee to keep her leg from jiggling. That gave her a moment to calm herself. "You've got my attention."

"I filled out the forms for my two friends." Blaise removed a folder from his computer bag. "I understand you don't want to travel. I assume because of your family, but you must come to Portland to meet them. I'll give you a one-hundred-thousand-dollar retainer. That should cover your expenses and time. I'm assuming you have a contract where you can change the amounts per your fee schedule."

His willingness to pay so much stunned her. It also didn't lessen her misgivings. "You want to win that badly?"

Blaise raised his chin. "I will win. It's a matter of when. With your help, it'll happen sooner."

She wasn't impressed by such a display of arrogance. Well, maybe a little. "Winning isn't everything."

He pushed back his shoulders. "Henry said the same thing, so let's agree to disagree."

She read through the paperwork. Blaise had filled out a form for each of his friends. Thoroughly. Yes, she wanted a larger house and doing this for Blaise would make that happen.

But this wasn't only about three million dollars. Her company's reputation was at stake. What if he was hiding something? About one or both men?

Hadley needed to make sure she could find them wives before she agreed. "I'll need to meet the two men before I say yes."

"You don't trust me when I say they're marriage material?"

"I don't know you."

His lips thinned.

"You have a vested interest in the outcome of the matchmaking beyond that of a caring friend," she continued, speaking at a fast clip. She hated how he made her nervous. "So, yes, I need to see for myself what your friends are like."

"You don't mince words and you're passionate about your work. I like that." Laughter glinted in Blaise's eyes, but something that looked like respect shone there, too. "Come to Portland on Sunday. You can meet Dash and Wes then."

Hadley straightened. "This Sunday?"

He nodded as if she could simply drive across the Bay Bridge to get there. Not fly there when she was due in New York on Monday morning.

"I'll invite everyone over to watch football," he added before she could speak. "Eat. Drink. Cheer on our teams. We've done it before."

"What will people think if I'm there?" she asked.

"My friends bring people over all the time."

"What about you?" she asked.

His gaze locked on hers. "I may not want a relationship or marriage, but I date casually."

She wondered about his type. Most likely sexy blondes with perfect hair and figures—the opposite of her. Dessert was her favorite food group. The extra sugar in her diet showed, but she wasn't about to starve herself to be a size two or four. Even six was pushing it because she enjoyed eating too much.

He raised a brow, the cocky gesture skyrocketing her pulse rate. "So, Sunday?"

No sat on the tip of her tongue until she pictured the Avila Street house from the Internet with four bedrooms and three-and-a-half bathrooms. There was even a backyard—albeit a small one. They could adopt a dog from the local animal rescue to keep Tiny company during the day.

Yes, no. Yes, no.

Logic battled with her heart, but practicality won over both. "I'll be there, but after I meet your friends, I reserve the right to say no."

"Deal, but bring whatever contract we'll need to sign to go forward." Blaise grinned as if he'd already won the bet. "Just in case you say yes."

Hadley was tempted to say yes now, but she couldn't. Finding someone a spouse was hard work. Many of her interviews weren't to take on clients, but with people who could be potential matches for them.

She skimmed over Blaise's paperwork. His two friends lived in Portland. Both had founded tech companies. One was in his mid-thirties. The other was in his late-twenties. It wouldn't be the first time she had clients not in the Bay Area or New York.

Finding wives for these men would be a means to an end. Could she, her sister, and the kids continue living in the condo? Yes, but a four-bedroom house would be more comfortable. That was her goal, what she was saving for.

Images from the house on the internet flashed through her brain. That was what she wanted—what her family needed.

So why was Hadley feeling so unsure? And why didn't she know if she wanted Sunday to go well so she could say yes or be a complete disaster so she could say no and never see Blaise Mortenson again?

Chapter Seven

After Blaise arrived in Portland, he found himself in one meeting after another because two from Monday had been crammed in between others. A typical day, except—he couldn't focus. He adjusted his glasses—his eyes needed time to recover before he wore contacts again—but his vision wasn't the problem.

He was distracted.

Which wasn't like him.

He quickened his pace. A few minutes alone in his office would help him regroup.

Trevor sat at his desk, staring at his computer monitor.

Blaise walked past his assistant and reached for the door handle.

"The contract you wanted is on your desk." Trevor glanced up at him. "I emailed you a pdf in case you prefer an electronic version."

"Thanks."

Trevor studied him. "You seem out of it. Do you need me to get you anything? Make you a doctor's appointment?"

The guy was perceptive. The quality could be both positive and negative. "Thanks, but I'm just not ready for Monday."

Trevor's mouth tightened. "It's Tuesday."

Oh, right. "My Monday was cut short, so that's where my brain is."

A partial truth. His mind wasn't here today. It was in San Francisco.

With Hadley.

"Was the trip to see Ms. Lowell worthwhile?" Trevor asked.

"Yes." More so than Blaise imagined it would be. "But nothing is firm yet."

That, he hoped, would happen on Sunday.

Hadley would get her money. He'd win the bet. Wes and Dash would thank Blaise for their wives.

Feeling better, he entered his office and closed the door behind him. It was only a matter of time.

When he'd mentioned the amount he was willing to pay Hadley, dollar signs had appeared in her pretty blue eyes. The way she'd gasped and then licked her lips showed her interest, but surprisingly, she hadn't given in to temptation.

That annoyed him and impressed him.

She was considering her company and what this might mean in the long-term, not doing a money grab.

All he needed was for Sunday to go well. He didn't care who showed up as long as Wes and Dash were there.

Which reminded Blaise.

He sat behind his desk and sent a text to Wes.

Blaise: *Did you see my message in the group chat?*
Wes: *I did.*
Blaise: *Will you be there?*
Wes: *Thinking about it.*
Blaise: *Just say yes.*
Wes: *I was thinking of spending the weekend in Hood Hamlet.*

Hood Hamlet, a small alpine-inspired town on Mount Hood, wasn't far—an hour-and-a-half drive from Portland, but that wouldn't do.

Blaise: *Come home early on Sunday or go next weekend.*
Wes: *What's the big deal? The season's just starting.*
Blaise: *We haven't gotten together in a while.*
Wes: *Mason is still on his honeymoon.*
Blaise: *Then we can do this again when he's back.*
Wes: *Fine, you convinced me.*
Blaise: *See you on Sunday.*

The contract Trevor mentioned was on Blaise's desk, but first, he wanted to ask Dash if he could hire Iris to plan the get-together. Wonderkid's high school best friend cooked, cleaned, and ran his personal life. More than once, and jokingly, Blaise had offered to double Iris's salary if she'd come work for him, but she claimed friendship trumped money. At least Dash let her help others when needed. Blaise needed her pulled-pork sliders on Sunday. He typed another text.

Blaise: *Did you see my message in the group chat?*
Dash: *No. Which group chat?*
Blaise: *The one you started with the six of us.*
Dash: *Sorry, mind elsewhere.*
Blaise: *On work or women?*
Dash: *Huh?*
Blaise: *Okay, work.*
Dash: *Always work.*
Blaise: *So football and food on Sunday?*
Dash: *Want Iris to cater?*
Blaise: *You're a mind reader.*
Dash: *Yours is easy to read.*
Blaise: *So Iris?*
Dash: *I'll tell her to call you.*
Blaise: *Does this mean you'll be there?*
Dash: *Since you're stealing my cook for the day, I have to show up or I'll starve.*
Blaise: *See you on Sunday.*

Now, Blaise was getting somewhere. He had the second person he needed to be at his house and a cook extraordinaire to prepare the food. The only person missing—his matchmaker. Might as well check in with Hadley, too.

Blaise: *Sunday is a go. Wes and Dash will be there.*
HL: *Great.*
Blaise: *Do you have any questions?*
HL: *I'll let you know after I finish my research.*
Blaise: *I'm here when you're ready.*

He waited for a reply but none came. She must be busy like him. Time to read through the contract.

The rest of the day, he kept waiting for her to reply. She didn't. Wednesday came and then Thursday. No text arrived from Hadley.

Was she still doing her research?

Blaise wanted to call, but he didn't want to come across as a creeper.

By Friday, he still hadn't heard from Hadley. On his way back to his office, he pulled out his cell phone. His patience had disappeared.

Contacting her wasn't crossing a line. He needed to discuss her visit on Sunday. That was business-related. Not personal.

Forget a text. Blaise would call. He clicked on her number.

One ring.

Her voice message announcement played. "You've reached Hadley Lowell. Please leave your name and number, and I'll call you back."

As Blaise disconnected from the call, he clenched his jaw. The other day when he'd texted people, he'd reached everyone when they were available to reply immediately. That wasn't the norm for his friends. Maybe it wasn't for Hadley, either. No reason to be frustrated. She would see he'd called and get in touch.

Except she didn't.

Each time he checked his list of calls and texts without seeing her name, his chest tightened.

A stupid reaction but he couldn't help it.

After listening to HR present about a new workplace inclusion training, he returned to his office. Still no reply from Hadley.

Okay, he hadn't left a message, but the call notification was often enough to get a reply. At least with his friends. Given she was flying to Portland this weekend, she should want to touch base and firm up plans. Unless...

Something happened to her or one of the kids.

His stomach churned.

He hit her number on his contact list.

One ring. Two... "Hello?"

Hearing her voice loosened his bunched muscles. "It's Blaise."

"What's up?" she asked as if hearing from him was no big deal.

It wasn't a big deal. Not really. Except he needed his pulse to calm. "I want to touch base about Sunday."

"I've booked my flight."

Blaise released the breath he hadn't realized he was holding. One step closer to winning the bet, but that wasn't on his mind as much as... "If you're flying in on Saturday, I could show you around. Take you out to dinner."

Ugh. Could he be any more obvious or awkward? If he kept this up, he would be competing against Dash for being the nerdiest with women.

"Thanks, but I'm not arriving until Sunday."

Blaise had no reason to be disappointed. She didn't need to be in town until then and wouldn't have to spend the night at a hotel. He had plenty of space, but offering his guest room *would* cross a line. The least he could do was be a friendly party host. "Do you need a ride from the airport?"

"No, thanks. I'm renting a car." She didn't miss a beat answering. "Text me your home address when you get a chance."

The rejection stung, which it shouldn't. This wasn't personal. "Did you finish your research?"

"Yes. I don't have questions about Wes and Dash, but I do have one about Sunday."

"Shoot."

Silence filled the line.

That was strange. "Hadley?"

"How should I introduce myself to your friends, especially Wes and Dash?"

Blaise leaned back in his chair. "Be yourself. If someone asks how we met, tell them Henry, which is the truth since he recommended you."

"Okay, I'll do that." Relief sounded in her voice. "I didn't want to lie to anyone."

"There's no reason to do that. You're in Portland for business." He wanted to put her at ease. "But no one will care why you're there."

"I hope you're right."

"I am." His confidence brimmed. This would work out as he planned. "Nothing to worry about. You'll see."

* * *

A quarter to noon on Sunday, Hadley stood at Blaise's front door. She straightened the bottom of her blouse—a Boho-inspired shirt she'd borrowed from Fallon—over a pair of dark jeans. The brown Chelsea boots coordinated with her crossover purse. It had taken her two hours to figure out what to wear.

Ridiculous.

The Craftsman-style house—okay, mansion might be a better descriptor—was in a swanky neighborhood. Nothing she hadn't seen in San Francisco or New York, yet her muscles twitched as if preparing for a race.

Back to the driver's side of her rental car.

She laughed because being so nervous wasn't like Hadley. Her clients were the elite. She knew the personality type better than most thanks to an ex-boyfriend, which was why she'd never been attracted to any of them.

Until Blaise.

Hadley clutched the handle of the gift bag she carried. Anything she felt for him was a crush, nothing more. Even if he wasn't a potential client, the difference between their worlds was vast.

Different galaxies.

This wasn't a fairy tale like her niece and nephew enjoyed watching. Nothing would ever happen between them.

She owned a business that paid her six figures and allowed her a condo in one of the most expensive real estate areas in the country. But he was willing to pay her two million dollars. Three, if she counted the bonus.

That kind of money was the stuff of dreams.

Yet it made their positions clearer—she would work for him. He was king of the hill, and she was a worker ant.

Which was why Hadley was here.

Not to see Blaise.

Meeting his two friends was the reason.

Ring the doorbell.

She reached toward the button, but her hand

froze, hovering inches away.

Misgivings swamped her.

Finding a person their perfect match without them being part of the process would be difficult. She could only ask so much. Based on her research, the two guys weren't stupid.

Her breaths rushed out in huffs.

Dash Cabot wasn't only the smartest one in the room. He was also one of the most intelligent people on this planet. He might be a nerd, but he dated. None of his relationships, however, appeared serious.

Wes Lockhart had graduated with an undergrad degree in engineering and an MBA. He was old money like Henry Davenport, but Wes had also been sick. He dated many women. One name had been mentioned more than the others, but she'd disappeared from his life around the time of his cancer diagnosis.

What if Wes and Dash figured out what Blaise wanted her to do? Would she and her company become the scapegoats? Billionaires had deep pockets with teams of lawyers. She didn't.

Nerves knocked louder than kids trick-or-treating on Halloween.

The situation had disaster written all over it.

If she left now, no one would know.

Three million dollars.

Like an echo in a canyon, the dollar amount swirled through her pounding head. She forced herself to slow her breathing. She needed the money to help her family. If she left—

The front door opened.

So much for making an escape.

"I saw you on the security camera." His warm smile turned her weak legs into linguini. "I wasn't sure if the doorbell was broken or if you were going to bolt."

His rich voice kicked her pulse up a notch. Or maybe it was how he was rocking the casual look in his khaki shorts, maroon Henley, and bare feet.

"Not bolting." She was breathless. That would work. "Catching my breath."

Before she hyperventilated, which could still happen.

She should have known a place like this would have a security system. That wasn't the worst part. She hated that her memory, even though she'd thought about Blaise all week, hadn't done his appearance justice.

Had the guy gotten hotter since Tuesday?

He raised an eyebrow, giving his features a rakish effect she shouldn't find so attractive. "Winded from your walk to the front door?"

Busted, but unless he called her out, she was admitting to nothing. "I'm good."

Hadley would be. She just needed a moment to prepare herself because she had no idea what to expect when she stepped inside. Being so far out of her comfort zone and having zero control was messing with her big-time.

Should have stayed home.

Too late now.

"This is for you." She handed him the gift bag, containing bars from a small-batch chocolate factory in San Francisco.

"Thank you." He peeked inside. "I've heard about this place. Two tech guys founded it. Are the chocolates as good as they say?"

"Better." She enjoyed going there. Or did before her caffeine moratorium. They sold chocolate bars, drinks, and pastries. "You can share with your guests or save for yourself."

His gaze narrowed. "Is this a test to see what I do?"

"If you wanted to hire me to find you a wife, it might be," she joked. "But since you don't…"

He laughed before motioning her inside. "Come in."

As she passed him, a whiff of his scent surrounded her.

Goose bumps covered her skin. The fragrance tantalized, making her want to inhale again. Maybe she should hold her breath when he was nearby, so she didn't get distracted. No, because what if she passed out? That would be worse.

She glanced into the living room. The décor was a comfortable mix of stained wood, buttery leather, and a few plaids. Masculine but not mancave. Not all shades of brown and ivory, either. Artwork provided splashes of color. The stacks of books and photographs added a touch of personality. But there was no mistaking the quality of the items.

"You have a lovely home," she said.

"Thanks." He glanced around. "Laurel Worthington Matthews deserves the credit. She's an interior designer."

Hadley recognized the name. "Laurel is a friend of Henry's."

Blaise nodded. "She and her husband, Brett, are here."

"Is Henry coming?"

"No, he's babysitting their daughter, Noelle. She was fussy this morning, so Henry stayed with her. Wes and Dash are also here. So are Adam Zeile, one of the six in the bet, and his wife, Cambria."

As they continued toward the back of the house, a delicious aroma filled the air. Hadley's mouth watered, reminding her she'd skipped breakfast this morning. "Something smells good."

Wicked humor lit Blaise's eyes. "Me or the food?"

She was tempted to say both, but this was a business meeting. No flirting allowed. "The food."

Her answer didn't dim his bright smile. "Then I hope you brought your appetite. I hired Dash's cook, Iris, to cater."

Hadley hadn't expected this to be like the potluck,

BYOB, game-watching parties she attended. Still, the hair at the back of her neck prickled. The last catered event she'd attended had been a wedding reception. "I can always eat. Even if the fit of my jeans tells me I shouldn't."

His gaze ran the length of her, slow and methodical as if not wanting to miss an inch. "Don't listen to your jeans. You look fantastic. There's nothing more attractive than a woman who enjoys eating more than rabbit food."

"Um, thanks." She stood straighter. That was the second time Blaise had complimented her. Okay, in roundabout ways. If she was here for another reason, she might think he was flirting. But she wasn't. "I get tired of salads fast but never cheeseburgers."

They entered a large open space with a kitchen, eating area, and family room. The pregame show played on a huge television screen. A man and woman sat on the large leather sectional. A guy in faded jeans and a hoodie lounged in a recliner, staring at his phone. Based on photos she saw during her research, that must be Dash. Movement outside the French doors caught her attention. Three people stood among the patio furniture and white canvas umbrellas.

This wasn't that much different from other gatherings.

Except most of the guests here were worth billions.

"Lunch is almost ready." A pretty young woman

checked inside the oven before wiping her hands on her apron. Her hair was pulled back in a low ponytail. Stray tendrils framed her face. Her black shirt and pants coupled with a pink apron gave off a Paris vibe. She extended her arm to Hadley. "Hi, I'm Iris."

"Hadley." She shook Iris's hand. "Everything smells so good. You must be quite a chef."

"Not a chef yet, but that's the dream." Iris grinned, exuding warmth. "For now, I keep Dash fed, his house cleaned, and his errands checked off his to-do list."

"I could use someone like you in my life," Hadley admitted.

"Me, too," Blaise agreed. "Too bad we can't clone you."

"No way. I'm one of a kind." Iris's green eyes twinkled. "So no talk of cloning when you tech guys, especially my boss, have the resources to pull it off someday."

A timer buzzed.

"That's my cue to serve lunch." Iris grabbed a hot pad off the counter. "Nice meeting you, Hadley."

"I'll talk to you later." Maybe Hadley could find out more from Iris about her boss, Dash.

"Come on." Blaise's hand rested at the small of Hadley's back. "I want to introduce you to everyone else."

His light touch was a friendly gesture, nothing more. Yet his warmth seeped through her shirt. "Lead the way."

"Wes is out on the patio."

The backyard was huge with a large manicured lawn. Small white bulb lights were strung across the patio which had both an outdoor kitchen and a firepit.

Wes Lockhart, whom she recognized from a photograph, stood next to a man and woman. The three appeared to be having a serious conversation. A sudden laugh transformed Wes's rugged features into movie-star attractiveness.

"Hey, guys," Blaise said to his friends. "I want you to meet Hadley. She's watching the game with us."

As they glanced her way, she smiled. "Hi."

"Nice to meet you, Hadley. I'm Wes." The man oozed charm. He was handsome with short brown hair and an easy smile. The lines at the corners of his eyes suggested he was a few years older than Blaise. "Are you a Seattle fan?"

"No," she admitted. "I'm a San Francisco diehard."

Wes placed his hand over his heart, staggered back a step, and glared at Blaise. "You invited her knowing this?"

Blaise grinned. "A blue-and-green love fest would be boring."

"Boring is my new favorite MO," Wes countered.

Interesting. Hadley wouldn't have expected him to say that from her research. Wes Lockhart had a cutthroat reputation. At least two articles suggested he was also an adrenaline-chasing sometimes-player, who made the most of his money, family connections, and free time. Maybe to counter that, he was a fan of "Netflix and chill."

"I'm Brett. Nice to meet you." A handsome man with dark hair and a trimmed beard shook her hand. "Don't mind Wes. He wants to be the twelfth man on the field, which means one day he'll buy the team or try to."

"I'd rather bring an expansion team to Portland," Wes chimed in. "The Rose City needs our own franchise."

Okay, this was a whole other level to what she was used to. Hadley and her friends talked about buying tickets to a game, not an entire team.

Brett raised his glass. "I'll be the first to sign up for a skybox."

"Boys and their football." A beautiful woman with caramel-colored hair rolled her eyes. "I'm Laurel. Forget what Wes said about your team. I root for Chicago, and they haven't kicked me out yet."

"Thanks." Hadley noticed Blaise had been quiet. "What team is your favorite?"

"Whichever is winning," he deadpanned.

The other two men laughed.

Wes shook his head. "Leave it to Mortenson. Losing isn't in his vocabulary."

A good thing his friends recognized that. Maybe

they would understand why Blaise wanted her to find them wives.

Laurel eyed Hadley curiously. "So how did you and Blaise meet?"

Hadley's mind went blank. A chill shot through her.

"Henry," Blaise answered.

Nice save, but Hadley didn't want to have to answer questions about them. Especially not in front of Wes. "Blaise told me you're his interior designer. It's lovely."

"Thanks." Laurel beamed. "I'm happy how the project turned out."

"And I'm thrilled how you turned the house into a home," Blaise chimed in. "I hope business is going well."

"Better than I hoped, but I'm trying to limit projects. My focus is Brett and Noelle."

Brett placed his arm around Laurel. "Until we have another."

Blaise's lips parted. "Wait, does this mean…"

Wes's eyes widened. "Are you—"

"Not pregnant. If I was"—Laurel raised her wine glass—"I wouldn't be drinking this."

Brett winked. "But we're preparing for when the time comes. Practice makes perfect."

The men laughed.

As Laurel shook her head, Brett pulled her closer. "You know it's true, my love."

Awww. Hadley swallowed a sigh. Henry was correct about these two. They were sweet together.

"I'll take Hadley inside to meet the others," Blaise said.

After three different versions of "talk to you later," Hadley followed him into the house. "They seem nice."

"They are." He glanced over his shoulder. "You'll need to spend more time with Wes."

"As long as I don't mention football, I should be fine."

"You'll do great."

His confidence buoyed her, making her feel they could pull this off.

The couple who'd been sitting on the couch when she arrived was in the kitchen with Iris. The guy—Dash—in the chair frantically tapped on his phone screen.

Blaise sighed. "Put away the game, Dash. It's time to be social."

Dash remained focused on his phone. "I'm not one to mingle unless it's through my headset during a game."

"Twenty-eight going on thirteen," Blaise whispered to her. "Come on, Dash. There's someone I want you to meet."

Dash glanced up. When his gaze met Hadley's, his face flushed. The game suddenly forgotten, he stood. He was taller than the other men with carelessly styled hair and attractive features.

"Sorry. I didn't realize anyone new would be here." Dash wiped his palms on his jeans and then shook her hand. "I'm Dash. The unsocial one still trying to figure out this thing called adulting."

She'd known he was younger than Wes and Blaise, but his clothes and mannerisms reminded her of a kid in college, trying to find his way. Must be more of a stereotypical tech guy. That put her at ease. She'd had other clients like Dash.

"Hadley," she replied. "It's nice to meet you, but sorry to take you away from your game."

"Oh, no worries."

For a nerd gamer, the guy appeared to be easygoing and friendly. That was a nice surprise.

"It's mine," he added.

"That means Dash wrote it," Blaise explained.

"Right," Dash said. "I was goofing around to see what score I could get since I haven't had time to play it for a while."

Definitely a different world. But Hadley didn't feel as uncomfortable as she thought she would. "I hope you did well."

"High score." Excitement filled his eyes. "But I know all the Easter eggs so I have an advantage. Oh, did you see the new personal sub going on the market? Might have to buy one."

Blaise shook his head. "Do you need a submarine?"

Dash shrugged. "Does Adam need a whiskey distillery or you a helicopter?"

"Touché," Blaise said.

Yep, these guys lived in another realm where money was no object.

She took in Dash from the top of his messy hair to his high-end tennis shoes.

Cute.

His long limbs reminded her of a puppy who was all legs. No doubt Dash had the same attention span. Get rid of his ultra-casual attire and put him in something nicer, say a suit, and he would be handsome. But she couldn't help him with a makeover as she would with other clients.

That could be a problem.

Dash's gaze traveled from her to Blaise. "We spent Saturday together at the wedding and you didn't say a word."

"About what?" Blaise asked.

"Hadley." Dash elbowed him. "Why didn't you tell me you were dating someone?"

Chapter Eight

As *dating* echoed through Blaise's head, Hadley tensed beneath his palm. He hadn't realized his hand was on her back. He jerked his arm away as if the action would defuse a ticking bomb. Not because he didn't enjoy touching her. He did. But Blaise didn't want to upset her more, because he saw that what Dash said had. "We're…"

"Friends," Hadley finished for Blaise.

"It's new," he added a beat later because Dash may have provided them with the perfect cover for their matchmaking.

Amusement gleamed in Dash's eyes. "Being friends is new? Or the two of you together?"

"Yes," Blaise and Hadley said at the same time.

That hadn't been on purpose. Though he had a

feeling they were each answering a different question.

Hadley gave him a wide-eyed what-are-you-doing look.

"You even talk at the same time. It's like Kieran and Selah all over again." Dash laughed before focusing on Hadley. "They're out of town celebrating their married-for-one-month anniversary, or they'd be here."

A charming pink stained Hadley's cheeks. Blaise hadn't expected her to be the blushing type, but it was cute. He enjoyed this glimpse of her flustered, but what he would prefer to see is her letting loose, acting spontaneous instead of holding on to control like a lifeline.

Her gaze, full of questions, remained on his. A hint of vulnerability shone through.

He fought the urge to run his finger along her jawline to see if her skin was as soft as it appeared to be.

Or as soft.

"Well, good for you guys," Dash said sincerely.

"Good?" Hadley's voice cracked. She glared at Blaise as if willing him to tell Dash, who remained oblivious, they were just friends, if that.

Blaise wished she wouldn't worry. Dash misunderstanding their relationship would help them in the long run.

Dash nodded. "Blaise keeps his personal life private unless we pry it out of him. The fact he invited you here is a good sign and telling."

It was true Blaise didn't share much, but he had his reasons. First, his childhood had sucked. If his friends knew what he'd been through with his drug-addicted parents, they would pity him. The way everyone else had while he was growing up. He didn't need or want that, but nowadays... "There's not much to tell when my life revolves around work."

"Revolved," Dash corrected. "Looks like that has changed thanks to Hadley. Which is great. You need a girlfriend."

Hadley flinched. "Blaise and I just met. We're—"

Dash whistled. "And you're here with his friends already? When you know, you know. That's what they say, right?"

"Who's ready for lunch?" Iris called from the kitchen.

"Let's go eat." Dash eyed the buffet set out on the island. "Iris made pulled-pork sliders."

As Dash headed to the food, Hadley grabbed Blaise's arm and leaned close to his ear. "Dash called me your girlfriend. Why didn't you correct him?"

The others congregated around the food. No one was paying attention to Hadley and him. "You're a girl—albeit a grown-up one—and a friend. So he's not completely wrong."

"Not. Funny." She ground out the words.

"You're right, but Dash has provided us the perfect reason for you being here."

Her mouth dropped open. "You seriously want to go with girlfriend?"

Blaise nodded.

"But it's not true. We're not…" The words shot from her mouth. "You agreed, no lies."

"We tried correcting Dash. He made his own assumptions."

"Semantics."

"Trust me."

"How can I do that when you're changing things as we go?" She lowered her voice. "In case you've forgotten, I haven't agreed to work with you."

"True, but you haven't said no, either." Blaise needed to be careful. He didn't want to upset her so she turned him down. "We'll talk after everyone leaves. Until then, please play along."

Her nostrils flared.

Best to leave her be for now. He walked away, moving toward the buffet. Everything would be fine.

Except as people settled in front of the TV to eat and watch football, the spot next to him, one where Hadley should sit, remained empty. She sat on the floor next to Cambria, Adam's wife. After lunch, Hadley retreated to the patio with Laurel. During halftime, she spoke with Wes and then moved on to talk to Dash.

Which was what Hadley was here to do.

So why did Blaise feel so…unsettled about her?

He grabbed a beer from the bar. His first of the

day and all because of Hadley. The liquid was cool and refreshing—his favorite local brewery.

"Hey." Laurel came up to him. "Where's Hadley?"

"Outside." He'd been keeping track of her, and his house wasn't that big compared to everyone else's.

"Hadley's great." Laurel glanced toward the doors leading to the patio. "Are the two of you serious?"

He gripped his beer. A good thing he was holding a bottle and not a can or he would have made a mess.

"We haven't known each other long." If he tried, he could calculate exactly how long. "We're still in the get-to-know-you stage."

Which he had never gotten to with any other woman.

A date or two was enough. Any longer and one might want him to open up and share his feelings.

And his past.

"Hadley mentioned you'd just met, but you're not one to invite people over."

"What do you mean? I invited all of you over today." He took another pull of beer. Sure, he was a loner, and he preferred it that way, but he tried to be friendly with those he knew. And Laurel had made the house perfect for entertaining.

"New people," she clarified.

Okay, that was true. Still, Blaise shrugged. He couldn't help it if he wasn't looking for new friends. The ones he had were good enough and could be trusted. Anyone else might have ulterior motives given his money.

Not that Hadley was here for any other reason besides the bet. He drank another sip, but it didn't quench him the way it had before.

Laurel straightened a stack of napkins. "I hope this works out."

"What?" he asked.

"You and Hadley." Laurel spoke as if it should be obvious. "She fits in nicely with everyone."

For now. Who knew the real Hadley?

Except he'd seen her with her niece and nephew during the day, at night, and in the morning. Maybe that *was* her.

Not that it mattered.

She was only here to speak with Wes and Dash so she could decide whether or not to accept Blaise's offer. Given her reaction before lunch, he had a feeling her answer might be no.

He swallowed around the lump in his throat. "Time will tell."

Laurel touched his shoulder. "There's no rush. Just see what happens."

"Is that code for take it slow?" he joked.

She nodded, glancing at her husband who was watching the game. "I say this as someone who ended up pregnant the night I met and married Brett during one of Henry's birthday adventures. Take it slow. Very, very slow. You'll be better off in the long run."

Blaise wasn't skilled at deciphering the hidden meanings in words. Numbers were his thing. But he had a feeling there was more she wasn't saying. "Things turned out well for the two of you."

"It took work. Patience. Anything good does."

"Sounds like you'll be the next author in the family."

Brett's two books on finances had hit the bestseller list. A single mom, who worked as a housekeeper for Henry Davenport's parents, had raised him. Brett had worked his way up from nothing. The same as Blaise, but the two had different investment strategies, which led to monthly and annual competitions to see which method—Brett's old-school research or Blaise's AI algorithms—worked best.

"You two can corner the market on nonfiction titles," Blaise added.

"Heavens, no. Writing doesn't appeal to me at all." Laurel shook her head as if to emphasize the point. "I was only giving you some friendly advice."

"Thank you." Not that Blaise would do anything with Hadley except pay her if she allowed him to hire her, but maybe someday he would need to remember what Laurel said.

The sound of Hadley's laughter drew his attention. He turned that way to see her speaking with Adam and Brett. Whatever she was saying had his friends captivated.

"You like her."

Blaise focused on Laurel. "I told you—"

"You're getting to know her. Got it." Humor danced in her eyes. "That doesn't mean you can't like her."

He shot a sideward glance Hadley's way. "She's smart and strong and stubborn."

Laurel's smiling face glowed. "I'll take that as a yes."

Instead of denying it—Blaise liked Hadley, except when she wouldn't do what he wanted—he drank more beer. He hadn't expected his friends to care this much about him dating anyone. All he'd wanted was an excuse if Hadley needed to speak with Wes or Dash again.

"I'll give you one more piece of advice from someone outside the inner circle," she added.

"You're part of the circle," he blurted.

"As a spouse and partner of someone who isn't at the same level as the rest of you."

Blaise frowned. He didn't understand where this was coming from, especially when he'd always felt like the outsider among their group. "That doesn't matter to us."

"Maybe not, because we're doing better each year, but it's still a little different." Laurel didn't sound offended. "The six of you and Henry are used to the world revolving around you, but that's not how it works for everyone else. Be nice to Hadley. If you keep dating her, and when whatever's going on between you two runs its course, let her down easy. Don't be the guy who breaks her heart."

"You mean like Wes."

"Before he got sick, yes. Adam, Mason, and Kieran used to be the same. Dash does it, too, but that's because he's clueless. You, however, are more evolved than the others. Don't be like them, okay?"

"Okay." Except Blaise wanted to be like the others. At the same time, he was trying to catch up and then pass them in net worth, but her words made him stand taller. "But you're missing out by not writing a relationship self-help book."

"Who's writing a book?" Hadley asked, coming up next to him.

About time. He smiled at her. "I told Laurel she should."

"I said no," Laurel said.

"Then start a podcast," he suggested with a wink before focusing his attention on Hadley. "Having fun?"

She nodded. "Thanks for inviting me."

He slipped his right arm around her, but she didn't come closer to him. "Glad you're here."

"The two of you should come to dinner this week." Laurel bit her lip. "Would Thursday work? I think that's the only day Brett is free."

"I'll check my schedule." Dinner sounded like fun to him. "Does that work for you, Hadley?"

Her jaw jutted forward. "I won't be in Portland, but thanks for the invite."

Blaise grimaced. How could he have forgotten that she wouldn't be in Portland during the week? "Hadley's business has offices in San Francisco and New York."

"We can do it another time." Laurel didn't hesitate replying. "I'm jealous, though. Our favorite bookstore is in San Francisco."

He blew out a breath, thankful Laurel hadn't asked more.

"Which one is that?" Hadley asked.

"Cassandra's Attic," Laurel said. "Brett's done book signings there."

Hadley's features relaxed. "I take my niece and nephew to story time there. It's a great bookstore."

"Small world. Say hi to Cassie and Troy from us when you're there next." Laurel picked up a brownie. "I'm going to watch the end of the game."

Hadley went to follow Laurel, but Blaise held on to her. He wasn't letting her get away yet. "Wait a minute."

"The game…"

"You can watch the highlights."

Everybody cheered. Something must have happened.

As she exhaled, her shoulders drooped. "What?"

"How's it going?"

She glanced toward the television, but her gaze

wasn't focused on the game. "Your friends are nice. Everyone cares a lot about you."

More shouts erupted.

Blaise didn't care. "Why do you say that?"

"I've never been asked so many questions in such a short time frame." She sighed. "I'm assuming your security team ran a background check on me. If so, let Wes know so he doesn't waste his time and money having one done."

Blaise laughed. "Wes can afford it. But he wouldn't..."

"I run them on clients. Credit checks, too. Based on his questions, that's what he's planning to do on me."

Okay, maybe Wes would. That should annoy Blaise but it didn't. "Wes acts like everyone's big brother. Always has."

"I can see that. Adam is more reserved, but he wouldn't stop pressing me about my job." Her mouth twisted. "Pretty sure he thinks I'm a gold-digger because of my vague answers."

Blaise shook his head. "Adam thinks everyone is a gold-digger. Well, except Cambria."

"Dash kept asking to see my phone," Hadley admitted. "You mentioned beta testing a tracking prototype so I wouldn't give it to him."

"He might have wanted to install a helpful app or fun game."

She lifted a brow. "If you say so."

"I do." Blaise hoped that was the case because sneaking tracking technology onto someone's phone would be creepy, no matter the motivation. "Did you find out what you needed?"

She nodded.

That didn't tell him anything.

"Blaise and Hadley," Wes called. "Only two minutes left in the game."

"Shall we?" Blaise asked.

His right arm still around Hadley, he stepped in her direction. She moved forward.

Oomph.

He collided into her, sending her stumbling backward.

Blaise held on to her with both arms. Somehow they both remained upright. She pressed against him. The rapid beat of her heart matched his. "It's okay."

Her breathing was faster than normal. "I thought I was going down."

"I've got you." Her face was so close to his. "I won't let you fall."

"Thanks."

He couldn't decipher the emotion in her eyes—gratitude, maybe—but her lips parted.

One taste.

That was all he wanted.

She seemed to want it, too.

He lowered his mouth to hers, and she met him halfway.

Warm. Soft. Home. The combination was potent. In that moment, he knew one taste would never be enough.

Blaise didn't care.

He moved his lips over hers, relishing the feel of them against his. She arched against him, her hands wrapping around him and her fingertips weaving their way through his hair.

"Nice catch!" Wes yelled.

Blaise tightened his hold on Hadley.

Yes, it was.

And no way was he going to fumble this.

* * *

Hadley was kissing Blaise. Or maybe he was kissing her. It didn't matter as long as the kisses continued.

The way his mouth moved over hers qualified as one of her best experiences ever.

Maybe *the* best.

Pleasurable sensations emanated from her mouth, shooting to the tips of her toes. And the way he tasted…

Her new favorite dessert.

Appetizer.

And main course, too.

"Only thirty seconds left!" a man shouted.

No, that was too soon for this to end. She wanted…more.

Someone moaned.

Her?

Didn't matter.

Hadley hadn't been kissed in…

She couldn't remember the last time, which told her it was a long time ago. These kisses, however, were worth waiting for.

"Blaise! Hadley!" someone else yelled.

The voice startled her.

Oh, no. She was kissing Blaise.

Hadley drew back.

"You don't want to miss the end of the game." That was Wes. Only she didn't dare glance his way. Not with her breathing uneven and heat rushing through her veins. Her lips felt swollen.

"You okay?" Blaise asked.

His ragged breaths matched hers. His face was flushed. Heat filled his gaze.

Hadley bit the inside of her cheek. She didn't go around kissing clients. Not that Blaise was one. At least not yet. Still, she didn't mix business with pleasure.

Or hadn't.

Until tonight.

Her lips tingled.

Was she supposed to feel regret or remorse?

Because she didn't. She hadn't known a kiss could be that good. Heaven help her, she wanted another one.

Blaise's eyes darkened. "Hadley?"

Oh, he'd asked her a question before saying her name. She nodded even though *okay* didn't describe how she was feeling at all.

"No!" Wes yelled.

"I can't believe they missed the field goal." That sounded like Adam or maybe Dash.

Blaise let go of her, but he didn't step away. Instead, he rested his forehead against hers. "I—"

"Get over here, Blaise." That was Brett's voice. "The game's going into overtime."

Blaise straightened before holding her hand, lacing his fingers between hers. "Let's watch the end of the game."

Football was the last thing on her mind. All she could think about was Blaise, the way he'd made her feel, and if the kiss meant anything to him.

Especially if she agreed to take him—well, Wes and Dash—on as clients. She'd never fallen for a client. Never been tempted even though some of the richest men—attractive men—had wanted to find wives.

Blaise sat on a leather love seat and pulled her down next to him, her hip and thigh pressing against his. After releasing Hadley's hand, his arm went around her, bringing her closer to him as if this were the most natural thing in the world, making her feel cherished and special, a way she hadn't felt in forever.

If anyone noticed them now or when they'd

kissed, no one said anything. All attention was focused on the game.

She should be relieved.

But her misgivings doubled with each passing second.

Blaise appeared unaffected while her nerve endings twitched and her lips demanded more kisses.

Not where she expected to find herself.

One kiss.

Not a big deal, right?

But her pounding heart rate hadn't quieted and told another story.

Play along.

Was that what this was about? A kiss for show?

Boulders settled in the pit of her stomach.

If that was the case—and why wouldn't it be—she'd played along as Blaise requested.

Perhaps, too much.

So what should she do next? Watch the game was a given. Ignoring the man plastered against her would be a smart move. But after everyone left, and it was just the two of them?

She didn't even want to think about that.

Chapter Nine

It was six o'clock. The game was over, and Blaise's friends had left. As Iris cleaned the kitchen, he sat on a stool, eyeing the French doors to the backyard. Hadley had stepped outside a few minutes ago. He was tempted to go out there, but he remained seated.

The reason?

He had no idea what to say to her if they were alone.

Just postponing the inevitable.

Yeah, so sue him.

Blaise wasn't a procrastinator, but he was doing it now. Being with Hadley brought a cyclone of emotions he wasn't ready to face.

Who was he kidding? He wanted it to stop.

Bet.

Girlfriend.

Kiss.

The day hadn't turned out as Blaise planned, but he wasn't sure how much he regretted doing or saying. He dragged his hand through his hair. What Hadley had to say, however, might change the way he felt.

Iris turned on the dishwasher. "I think that's everything."

"You did too much, as usual."

He envied Dash for having a trusted, loyal childhood friend work for him. Blaise's only friends growing up had been two employees at his high school. His math teacher, Mr. Penney, helped Blaise apply to college and let him work in his classroom after school so he wouldn't have to go home. The custodian, a grizzly guy named Coop, caught Blaise using one of the school's master keys to store stuff in the janitor's closet so his parents couldn't sell it to buy drugs. Coop had taken the key, but he offered Blaise a new place to store his things, one that wouldn't get him in trouble.

Which is why he'd bought each a new car and a vacation home long before Blaise had traded in his old Honda sedan and bought a house for himself. The two men, his only links to the past, still checked in on him, more like surrogate uncles than the mentors they'd once been. Occasionally, not as often these days because of Blaise's schedule, the three met for coffee or a meal. The way they had when he was in college and working two jobs to support himself. They'd rotated paying back then. Blaise picked up every tab now.

"You hired me." The determination in Iris's eyes matched the set of her jaw. "The only way to do a job is to give it your all."

"Which is what you always do." Blaise grabbed an envelope from a nearby drawer and handed it to her. Inside was money to pay for her expenses and her services plus a bonus. "Robyn won't have anything to do when she arrives tomorrow morning."

"This house is huge. Your housekeeper will have plenty to clean. I never went upstairs." Iris placed the envelope in her bag. "I didn't mop or vacuum down here, either."

"Go before you do that."

Iris glanced around. "Where's Hadley?"

That was the question Blaise had asked himself whenever he couldn't see her. He knew the answer this time. "Out on the patio."

"I like her."

That had been a common refrain today. A few had warned him not to mess up with her. Adam, however, had withheld judgment, which must have been difficult since he had an ulterior motive for wanting Blaise to fall in love and get married so the bet would be called off and the money divided amongst the six of them.

So not happening. "She's nice."

"Nice, huh?" Iris removed two containers he didn't recognize from the refrigerator and placed them in a box. "That's how you describe Hadley after sharing a scorching kiss?"

The kiss had been hot. He wanted another one. "Hadley is nice. Everybody agrees."

"This should be fun to watch." Iris laughed. "See you around. And Hadley, too."

Blaise escorted Iris out and watched her car back out of the driveway before returning inside.

The only sound was the dishwasher running. A big difference from an hour ago with the post-game show playing on the television and people talking over the sports analysts.

He sat on the couch. This was as good a spot to talk to Hadley as any. The only problem? He had no idea what to say to her.

Weird.

He usually wasn't at a loss for ideas or words. Most often, before others realized there was an issue or a problem, he had a solution figured out. That was why he got along so well with his friends. The six of them were similar. Brett, too. Henry could be when he tried, but the guy kept them entertained.

Hadley, however, had crashed the network in Blaise's brain. He'd rebooted, but his synapses weren't functioning normally, and he had no idea what to do about it.

She stepped inside from the patio and closed the door. "Everything's clean outside."

"Iris must have taken care of it earlier. She left."

"Oh." Hadley glanced around, rubbing her thumb across her fingertips. "Is there anything else that needs to be done?"

"If there is, I have people who will take care of it tomorrow." He patted the cushion next to him. "Come join me."

Her expression pinched, but she did as he asked. "So…"

Blaise wasn't ready to talk about the kiss. He'd start with the reason she was here. "What did you think of Wes?"

She blinked slowly as if not expecting that question. "Wes is charming and handsome. Not to mention smart but not in a talk-over-your-head way. Given he's the heir to one of the wealthiest families in the country, he checks all the boxes."

"Yours?" The question shot out before Blaise could stop it.

Hadley lifted her chin with defiance gleaming in her eyes. "I don't date clients."

Just kiss them.

No, that wasn't fair. Blaise had kissed her first. "Wes isn't a client."

At least not yet.

"No, but I'm not interested in him."

That wasn't enough information for Blaise. "Not

your type?"

"I don't have a type, but many women would call Wes a catch." Hadley tilted her head. "I wasn't able to dig too deep into his past or his future plans. If I had, he would have known something was up, so there are unanswered questions where he's concerned. But I learned a few things about him I didn't know."

That was good. "What about Dash?"

A smile lit up her face. "Dash is funny. He bounces from gamer boy to genius nerd in seconds. If I didn't know he was twenty-eight, I'd say he was in his early twenties. Social skills aren't his strength, but I'm guessing he's occupied by other things he deems more important than chitchat since he's quick to warm up and talk when that's necessary. I thought he was sweet."

"Even when he called you my girlfriend?"

Her cheeks reddened. "Well, other than that. But I am concerned…"

Was she attracted to Dash? Sweat dampened the back of Blaise's neck. "What?"

"He and Iris. They act like a couple when they're together."

"They've been best friends since high school. That's all."

Her nose wrinkled. "You're sure?"

Blaise nodded. "Dash can be oblivious, but friends are important to him. That includes Iris. He'd be lost without her. She keeps him in line."

"Sounds like more than a friendship."

"It's not." Blaise spoke with confidence. "The only games Dash plays are video or board games. If something *was* going on between them, we'd know. Everyone would know."

"I believe you. And that's good because an attractive, successful geek worth billions also checks many boxes."

Blaise had a similar nerdiness but kept that hidden. Would Hadley be interested in that side of him?

He wasn't sure he wanted to know the answer. "Does that mean you'll add them to your client list?"

"I didn't say that, but I'm considering it."

Relief poured through him. "What more do you need to say yes?"

"We need to talk about what happened tonight first."

Blaise's throat tightened. That was the last conversation he wanted to have, but he had no choice. "Do you want an apology?"

"Are you sorry you let people think we're dating?" she said at the same time.

He opened his mouth but then pressed his lips together. There were two answers—the truth and what she wanted to hear. But she had said no lies. Her being called his girlfriend and them pretending to date were enough. He couldn't add to that. "I'm not sorry."

"I had a feeling that would be your answer."

"It made things easier."

"Tonight, maybe."

At least she acknowledged that.

"What happens now that people believe we're together?" she asked. "We live in different states. People will soon realize we spend no time together."

"Lots of people have long-distance relationships. Texts, calls, video chats. It's no big deal. Besides, San Francisco isn't that far away."

"True, but don't forget I alternate weeks between my two offices. I have to catch a red-eye to New York in a few hours."

He straightened. "You're going tonight?"

She nodded. "I have a meeting tomorrow morning."

Which offered further explained why she couldn't be here to have dinner with Laurel and Brett on Thursday. But Blaise didn't like Hadley being so far away.

Wait. What was he thinking? None of this was real.

"We don't have to explain the time we spend apart. No one will know or care." His friends were too busy to keep track of him. "If anything, your job means we have a built-in reason why we're not together much. The only time any of them would see us is if you need to find out more about Wes or

Dash."

"So we're dating in name only."

That brought a laugh. "Yes, tonight was the first of a limited number of appearances, depending on how much you need to see Wes and Dash in person."

She tilted her head as if considering everything. That frustrated him because he made decisions quickly, but he knew most people weren't like him. And Hadley had slow and steady written all over her.

She tapped her finger against her chin. "What about the kiss?"

Here we go. Blaise swallowed. He should have known she wouldn't forget that. "Kissing provided evidence that we're together."

Her gaze narrowed, but that didn't hide the wariness in her eyes. "So the kiss was for show?"

His palms sweated. The kiss hadn't been premeditated. He didn't like that she thought it was. "The kiss just sort of happened when I found you in my arms, but it worked out well."

"Because others saw us."

It wasn't a question. "I'm sorry for not asking you first."

But he wasn't sorry for the kiss itself.

"No apology required," she said to his relief. "I will need access to Wes and Dash. As long as you downplay the girlfriend angle to your friends and we don't kiss again, it should be okay."

He blew out a breath, except…

Don't kiss again.

A heaviness pressed against Blaise, making him feel as if he held weights on each shoulder. He broke eye contact to avoid her seeing his disappointment about no more kissing.

"Because I don't kiss clients," she added.

He considered her words. "Does that mean you'll be my friends' matchmaker?"

She nodded.

"But I'm the client, not them?" He wanted confirmation on that point.

"You're paying me so you're the client."

Okay, no more kisses. Maybe once his friends were married…

Blaise shook the thought from his head. He was getting ahead of himself. "Thank you."

"Don't thank me yet." Her voice was strained. "I want to be on record saying this is most likely going to blow up in both of our faces."

"It won't."

"I wish I had your confidence."

Hard work and letting his tunnel vision drive him until he accomplished what he'd set out to do had led to success, from graduating high school to attending college to founding his own company. He was doing the same thing with the bet by finding the one person who could help him win sooner. "Trust me."

* * *

Trust me.

Sitting on the airplane, Blaise's words sounded in Hadley's head. The way they had since she'd left his house. The only-in-her-imagination voice teased and mocked her.

Forget about him.

Other passengers were still boarding. Hadley had a window seat. She adjusted the air stream above her before she tugged on her seat belt to make sure it was secure. Even though she flew to the East Coast twice a month, she scanned the aircraft safety card, located her closest emergency exits, and then shoved the instructions into the seat pocket in front of her.

Trust me.

The voice was back.

Hadley didn't trust Blaise. She couldn't.

Winning isn't everything.

Henry told me the same thing, but let's agree to disagree.

Blaise wanted to win. He would stop at nothing to get what he wanted, doing or saying anything, no matter what the cost. Earlier today, he'd let his friends believe he was dating her, kissing her to prove they were together, even if he claimed not to have planned that.

Who knew if that was true?

She couldn't trust him.

Wouldn't.

Even if her lips wanted more kisses.

And you, too.

No, Hadley didn't.

Client, remember?

Her cell phone rang. She glanced at the name on the screen—Blaise.

That was strange. "Hello?"

"Boarding the plane?" he asked.

Chills—the good kind—shot down her arms. Not good. And then she realized what he'd asked. Her fingertips dug into her phone case. "Did Dash put a tracking device on my phone?"

"No, but I've taken that flight before."

Silence filled the line. Uncomfortable and awkward. She cleared her throat. "Did you want something?"

"Your retainer will be deposited first thing in the morning."

She didn't know Blaise well, but the man seemed anything but forgetful. "You told me that two hours ago. What's going on?"

More silence. No music or television played in the background. If she listened hard enough, Hadley wondered if she would hear the gears turning in his brain. "Blaise?"

"I need you in Portland this weekend."

She couldn't have heard him correctly. "What did you say?"

"I need you to come to Portland this weekend.

Well, Saturday night."

A million thoughts ran through her head. They'd discussed how they would downplay their dating. "Why? I'm not supposed to come back unless I need to talk with Wes or Dash."

"Change of plans."

Oh, no. Was this something he'd planned to happen? Had everything he'd said earlier been lies?

"You need to explain because this is the opposite of what we decided at your house." Her voice was firm, hard. "That was only a couple of hours ago."

"Kieran and Mason will be around this weekend." Blaise hesitated. "They want to meet you."

She'd heard the names today, but it made little sense. "Isn't Mason on his honeymoon? And the other guy away for his one-month anniversary?"

"Yes, but both called me after you left. Not texted. Called. They never do that. Word about my new girlfriend got around fast."

Girlfriend, not date. Hadley nearly groaned. "I signed on as a matchmaker, and we have a plan. It included downplaying the whole dating scenario. I don't want to deceive your friends more."

"Me, either. I had no idea people would be so interested in my dating life. Honest." Blaise sounded sincere, but pretending had been his idea so what did she know? "Kieran and Mason are the only ones who haven't met you. After Saturday, we can do as we planned and not be seen together much."

That didn't make her feel better.

"But I'm not your…" She couldn't bring herself to say it. "This is ridiculous."

"It is." Blaise laughed.

She would have to keep her voice low. "It's also not funny."

"You're right. I'm sorry."

Hadley had a hard time believing that. A man put a rollaway suitcase into the overhead bin and then sat on the aisle seat of her row. "Are you?"

"You have no idea."

Hadley did, because of the regret she heard in each of his four words. Blaise needed her skills as a matchmaker. But he was stuck with her being his "girlfriend." It was a means to an end.

She could tell that.

Someone like him would never date her.

Hadley wasn't being negative or getting down on herself. She knew this because she'd been in this position before—being used prior to getting tossed aside.

It hadn't been fun. Her ex-boyfriend in college had begged her to write his papers and do his homework so he wouldn't be benched. Once the football season ended, he'd dumped her. There had also been the rich guy who'd only dated her to make another woman jealous. Not to mention the coworker at her job at an online dating firm who'd used her crush on him to claim her hard work as his own and be offered the promotion she'd wanted.

The difference this time?

You could have said no and never seen him again.

Except she hadn't.

She'd gone into this with her eyes wide open and said yes because Blaise was paying her. An amount she hadn't even dreamed about earning.

She needed to stop complaining and make this work. For both of them. "Will Wes and Dash be there on Saturday?"

"I was so surprised by the invite I didn't ask, but I can find out." Blaise spoke faster than normal, suggesting she wasn't the only one who was nervous. "We won't stay long. No kissing or holding hands. I'll charter a jet so you can travel at your convenience."

Uncertainty gnawed at her, but she couldn't give in to it.

Instead of dwelling on those feelings, Hadley closed her eyes. She imagined that house on Avila Street and the thirty-eight photos of the interior and exterior. With what Blaise would pay her and the equity from selling the condo, she could afford it.

What choice did she have?

Hadley took a breath. And another. "I'll be there."

Chapter Ten

On Friday, Blaise's cell phone buzzed with notifications. A strategically leaked rumor about the new fund earlier in the week had resulted in a frenzy of calls and messages.

Not that he was in a rush to answer.

The goal had been to fuel anticipation. They'd succeeded.

As he grabbed his phone to silence it, two initials on the screen made him do a double take.

HL.

Blaise hadn't heard from her. Not that they'd planned to stay in touch this week, but he'd thought about her. More than he'd wanted to acknowledge.

Was it guilt for what happened on Sunday and what he was asking for this upcoming Saturday?

Or perhaps gratitude for everything extra she was doing?

Maybe a combination.

He unlocked his screen and pulled up her text.

HL: *Could we reschedule dinner? Been fighting a cold all week. I don't want to spread germs.*

Blaise: *We could, but didn't you want to talk with Wes and Dash?*

No dots showed up indicating she was typing a response. But he had an idea.

Blaise: *How about we make it an early night so you can get to bed early? A good night of sleep might be all you need.*

HL: *I am tired.*

Blaise: *We'll appease my friends. Get the info you need. Eat. Then leave.*

HL: *That's better than a full evening out. But don't blame me if you get sick.*

Blaise: *If you've had this all week, I'm sure you're no longer contagious. And since we won't be kissing, I'll take my chances.*

HL: *Okay. My sister will be happy I won't be home to re-infect them. The kids had colds last week. See you tomorrow at your house.*

As Blaise reread the texts, his shoulder muscles loosened, the knots softening. The tension in his face eased. Funny how Hadley could frustrate him yet also relax him. He looked forward to seeing her again.

He hated that Hadley didn't feel well. Her worrying about getting others sick didn't surprise him. Even if her concern was unfounded. Sniffles, sneezes, and coughs were common in the fall.

On Saturday morning, Hadley texted him that her flight was delayed so she would go straight to his house and change there instead of the hotel she'd booked. He worked out, trying to expel the extra energy he'd woken up with, and had brunch at a small café with Mr. Penney and Coop.

After that, Blaise went home where he worked for a few hours, changed clothes, and then waited for Hadley to arrive. The house was spotless, though it usually was. All he had to do was put an empty glass in the sink. He tried to read, but the words blurred on the page. A press of the remote brought the television to life. A college football game. That would do for now.

Blaise checked the time during each commercial break.

Hadley should have been here by now. They weren't running late yet, but where could she be?

He pulled up a flight app, only to close it. He didn't know what airline she'd taken so he couldn't look up her arrival time. Given her earlier text, he assumed she would have let him know if her flight had been delayed more. Maybe she hit traffic on the drive from the airport.

He pulled up another app that displayed the roads in the area. A few spots showed red, signaling a delay, but most of the freeway was green.

The doorbell rang.

His pulse kicked up.

Blaise went to the door, forcing himself not to hurry, and opened it.

Hadley stood with tired eyes and a suitcase next to her. She wore a long sweater over a T-shirt, faded jeans, and short boots. Her hair was pulled back in a loose, lopsided ponytail. The edges of her lips curved in a closed-mouth smile. "Hi, Blaise."

His stomach did a somersault. He didn't know if it was her clothes, her smile, or how she said his name. "Hey, you made it."

"I did." She glanced at her luggage. "I don't have a smaller bag with me to hold my clothes for tonight, so I'm stuck lugging this around."

"I'll get it for you."

She sniffled. "Thanks."

He picked up her suitcase. "Still fighting the cold?"

She nodded. "I slept most of the flight. It's almost time for more cold medicine. I'll be good to go for dinner."

He motioned her inside. "I'll show you to one of the guest bedrooms. There's a bathroom attached. All the towels are clean, if you want to shower."

"Thanks." Hadley rubbed her forehead. "A

162

shower might clear the sinuses."

She followed him upstairs without saying a word. Must have been a long flight. Or maybe a rough week.

"Did you add any new clients in New York?" he asked when they reached the second floor.

"No, I limit the number of clients, and my roster is full thanks to you."

"Then why were you there?"

"To meet with potential candidates and check in with my clients. Some need more help than others with dating and romance." She yawned. "Excuse me. I'm a little tired."

"What kind of help?"

"Clothes, social skills, dating, the list is varied and unique."

"Do you do this for both the clients and the candidates?"

"I do whatever is necessary to find my clients a spouse perfect for them. My cold didn't hit until Monday night, so I was still able to do a practice date."

Imagining her on any kind of date, including a practice one, bugged him. "Did it go well?"

She nodded, her smile widening. "He did much better than the last time."

"Good for him." But how could a guy not know how to date?

An image of Dash flashed in his head.

Never mind.

She coughed into the crook of her elbow. "Sorry. I need another dose of cough medicine."

Hadley was also congested and glassy-eyed. She needed to be in bed, resting, not dragged to a private supper club. They could stay home. Order takeout for dinner. That might be a smarter plan. "Maybe we should cancel."

"I thought you said we'd make it an early night?"

He had, except... "You're tired and don't feel well."

She shrugged. "I thought I was doing better, but I think traveling wore me out. You want to go, right?"

Blaise did, but now he was torn. Both over the dinner and her staying at a hotel when she didn't feel well.

She spent this week in one.

True, but she likely had no other option in New York. Here...

"We'll leave before dessert," she suggested. "Okay?"

He thought he'd feel more relief at her wanting to go. Maybe he was tired, too. Still, the dinner was important for two reasons. She could find out more info about Wes and Dash. Introducing her to Kieran and Mason tonight also would keep her from having to return to Portland before she was ready.

Not that seeing her was a hardship for Blaise.

"That works," he said finally. "I'll be in the family room. Watching football. While you get, uh, ready."

Blaise fought the urge to cringe. He sounded stupid. She didn't care what he was doing or why.

"Is Lex going with us?" she asked.

"He's off this weekend. Rizzo's on. He'll drive us to the restaurant." Blaise glanced from her to the door of the bathroom. "Let me know if you need anything."

Not that he had a clue where to find something. A new tube of toothpaste and other toiletries appeared when his ran low. He assumed Robyn took the same care with the guest rooms in case he had visitors. Which he never did, but why not be prepared?

Hadley's shoulders slumped, making him think she needed sleep more than a shower.

"Are you sure you're up for tonight?" he asked.

She nodded. "It won't take me long to get ready."

Thirty minutes later, they were on their way.

Rizzo glanced in the rearview mirror of the SUV, his dark chocolate gaze on Hadley. "Do you feel okay?"

"I have a cold." She slouched in the back seat. "I'm waiting for the medicine to kick in."

Where Lex was bleach-blond and fair-skinned, Rizzo had jet-black hair and an olive skin tone. Both men, however, were inked and could go from relaxed to intense faster than Kieran's newest thoroughbred horse ran down the straightaway at Belmont.

"O-T-C?" Rizzo asked.

She yawned and then blinked as if trying to keep her eyes open. "Yes."

Blaise fought the urge to offer his shoulder as a pillow, but they didn't have far to drive. He was also trying to sort through the mix of emotions being with Hadley brought to the surface—concern, protectiveness, respect, attraction.

Rizzo focused on the road. "Drink water tonight. Not alcohol. You want to stay hydrated."

Hadley turned away from Blaise and then coughed. "Sounds like a plan."

"It is," Blaise agreed. "Rizzo is a trained medic."

Rizzo nodded. "Have questions or need advice, I'm your man."

"Medical ones, you mean?" she asked.

Glancing in the rearview mirror again, Rizzo winked. "Whatever you need."

Was the bodyguard flirting with Hadley?

Blaise's stomach burned. The guy was friendly, more so than Lex, but that was because of Rizzo's outgoing personality. Both Laurel and Cambria had mentioned Rizzo was attractive. Iris, too. Would Hadley think so?

Doesn't matter. She's not your real girlfriend.

True, but Blaise wanted the logical part of him to be quiet and let him be indignant.

You mean, jealous.

Shut up.

He couldn't believe he was arguing with himself.

"Have you spoken to Dash or Wes this week?" she asked.

At least she wasn't flirting back. "Wes called to get a rundown on you. You were correct about his wanting to run a background check. I talked him out of it. Dash and I texted. Everyone is crazy busy. Especially me."

Blaise was rambling, which was unlike him. He didn't share much about his personal life, but something about being with Hadley sent the words gushing like water from a broken water main.

"Busy is your normal, right?" She sounded more amused than upset.

Good, that meant she was feeling better. "Yes. I get antsy if I don't have enough going on."

"Overachievers are like that. Guessing you and your friends have that in common." She coughed again. "You mentioned Dash isn't seeing anyone, but he must have women who are interested in him."

"He does, but dating isn't a priority, so he lets them do the pursuing."

"That will make things easier."

"Dash prefers easy," Blaise explained. "He has a few nicknames. Wonderkid. Midas. The other is Mr. Status Quo because he's not a fan of things changing or fond of conflict. He'll do whatever it takes to avoid both."

"Good to know," Hadley said. "All these snippets

of info will help me find the right match for him."

Rizzo pulled into a parking spot near the restaurant.

"Do you feel the same as Dash about change and conflict?" she asked.

"I like change. I thrive on it." Blaise thought about his battle with the board and issues with employees. "Conflict isn't something I seek, but somehow it finds me."

Rizzo escorted them into the restaurant before disappearing. Most likely to the bar, where he could drink a soda and watch the door. At least that was what Lex had done when Blaise went out with friends.

The interior was dark with brick walls, hardwood floors, and overhead lights strategically placed. Flickering candles in jars provided more atmosphere than illumination. A din of customers' conversations sounded over instrumental music.

A hostess led them to a private dining space. Three couples sat at the large square table. Only two spaces on one side remained empty. What about...

"Where are Dash and Wes?" Blaise asked, trying to keep his voice steady.

"Wes is spending the weekend in Hood Hamlet," Adam said.

Kieran lowered his pint of beer. "Dash is at a video game conference."

Blaise muttered under his breath. He shot a

pointed look at Mason. "You said everyone would be here."

"I thought they would be." Mason's smile was more of a smirk.

Blaise's throat constricted. He and Hadley should have stayed home tonight.

"What does it matter?" Mason asked. "They met your girlfriend on Sunday. Now it's our turn. Hadley, isn't it?"

"Hadley Lowell," she said without missing a beat. If she was disappointed Wes and Dash weren't here, she didn't show it. "Are you Kieran or Mason?"

Everyone introduced themselves. Mason, of course, went first and then his wife, Rachael. Next was Kieran and his wife, Selah.

Adam leaned back. "Good to see you again."

Cambria motioned to the empty chairs. "Take a seat."

Hadley sat first and then Blaise did. Remembering what Rizzo had said in the car, Blaise poured her a glass of water and handed it to her.

She stared up at him through her eyelashes. "Thanks."

His heart bumped.

"It's great to meet you, Hadley." Mason placed his arm around his wife. "None of us knew Blaise was dating someone or we would have invited you to our wedding."

"It's new," Blaise answered for her.

She nodded in agreement. "No plus-one necessary."

Blaise smiled at her, pleased how she fit in right away. The same as she had on Sunday. "Not yet, anyway."

"Must be hard," Mason said.

"What do you mean?" Blaise asked.

"A long-distance relationship." Mason's smirk returned which meant one thing—he was up to something. "Not sure how you manage it. Especially with Hadley's matchmaking firm having offices in New York and San Francisco. When do you see each other?"

Blaise froze. A simple search would pull up Hadley's information, but he hadn't expected Mason to be so nosey. That wasn't like the guy. And then Blaise remembered the garter toss. This must be his friend's way of getting even. He sighed.

Brought this on myself, but winning the bet will be worth it.

The person he felt bad for was Hadley. He got that his friends would have questions, but she didn't deserve an inquisition.

"You created the Talk-View-Text app, right?" Hadley asked before Blaise could say anything.

Mason beamed like a proud daddy. Talk-View-Text, AKA TVT, was one of the hottest social media apps on the market. The success of the IPO had shocked everyone. "I did."

"Now his head will be even larger," Adam teased.

Kieran laughed. "He's catching up to yours."

If Hadley heard what they said, she ignored it. Instead, she smiled at Mason. "Then you should know how technology allows people to be together no matter the distance. Thanks for making it easier for us to see each other when we're miles apart."

Mason swallowed before lowering his hand from around Rachael. "You're welcome."

Everyone chose that moment to take a drink. Selah, who worked at Mason's company, appeared as if she was trying hard not to laugh.

Hadley impressed Blaise. Not only had she held her own against Mason—not an easy thing to do when the guy was on a roll—she'd also saved Blaise from saying something he would regret.

His gaze met hers, her blue eyes drawing him in. Resisting their appeal was futile.

Something passed between them, a connection— maybe an understanding—but he didn't feel as if he were on his own. Warmth spread through him, bringing with it an unfamiliar sense of contentment. Strange, because he had everything he wanted. Well, except for winning the bet. Maybe that was why he felt so close to her.

Blaise covered her hand with his. Her skin was

soft and warm.

Hadley's gaze never wavered from his, and he wasn't about to break the contact himself.

And then he remembered…

No kissing or holding hands.

He gently squeezed her hand before letting go. It was the right—the only—thing for him to do, but he missed the contact.

Blaise flexed his fingers, which itched to touch her once again. He knew better than to do that, but there was something else he could do. He needed to clear the air with Mason or the night would go downhill.

"Thanks from me, too, Mase." Blaise smiled at his friend because they were friends no matter their bets, competitions, one-upmanships, or arguments over the years. The same as he was with Adam, Kieran, Wes, and Dash. The six of them understood each other— the work, the money, the challenges—as few others could. "I'll pick up the tab tonight. It's the least I can do since I didn't pick up the garter at your wedding."

The nods and smiles around the table told Blaise he'd said the right thing.

"No hard feelings?" he asked.

"None. Especially now that Hadley's here." Mason raised what looked to be a glass of bourbon. "Has Blaise mentioned the bet to you?"

She nodded.

"Good." Mason glanced at Blaise. "We have less than nine months left to get the bet called off. Since it appears you're off the market now, maybe Hadley can use her expertise to find women for Dash and Wes."

This time it was Hadley who reached for her water glass and drank, but that didn't stop her gaze from colliding with Blaise's.

He winked at her. "Maybe she can."

Chapter Eleven

Blaise, Adam, Kieran, and Mason picked on each other, joking more like brothers than friends. Underneath the ribbing, however, was a bond Hadley envied. She had friends, but work and her family took up most of her time. Not that she minded. Fallon was not only her sister but also her best friend, but maybe Hadley should keep in better touch with other friends. Not everyone lived nearby, but as she'd mentioned to Mason earlier, technology made keeping in touch simpler. Friendship, however, was easy to take for granted. Yet somehow these men, including those not here tonight, had managed despite their busy lives and work.

The three women were friendly and got along but weren't as close as the guys. That made sense because they hadn't known each other as long. She enjoyed talking to them, especially Cambria after meeting her on Sunday, but Hadley struggled to keep up with the many topics being discussed. Her brain was fuzzy. Must be the cold medicine.

Kieran made a joke about nanotechnology, and Blaise couldn't stop laughing. He bent over slightly, laughter pouring out of him and wrapping around her like the best hug ever.

Hadley's breath caught in her throat.

He was handsome—okay, gorgeous—but seeing him so carefree filled her stomach with flutters. Tonight with his friends melted away the tension she'd noticed in the set of his shoulders and jaw when she'd arrived at his house. He'd given her a glimpse of a more relaxed Blaise on last Sunday, but he was out in full force now. She might have wanted to cancel, but she was glad they'd come tonight. This dinner—being around his friends—was good for him.

She drank her water, trying to stave off more coughs. That only made her shiver. Goose bumps prickled her skin. The water hadn't tasted that cold. Maybe the restaurant lowered the thermostat. She had her arms over her chest, wishing she hadn't left her sweater at Blaise's house.

Maybe food would help.

Hadley speared a scallop with her fork, but the thought of raising the bite to her mouth felt like too much effort. What she tasted had been delicious, but her appetite had vanished.

Rachael mentioned a hit television show. Or maybe they were talking about a movie.

Hadley blinked, trying to refocus so she could pay more attention to what people were saying. Voices droned on, making her feel like an observer from afar, not a participant seated at the table.

Someone mentioned a CEO's woes and being asked to step down from his position even though he'd founded the company.

"Shouldn't have gone public," Blaise said in a matter-of-fact tone.

Kieran shook his head. "Sometimes there's no choice."

Exhaustion clawed its sharp talons into her, poking holes and draining Hadley's energy like a faucet left running at full blast. All she wanted was to sleep.

She stifled a yawn.

Another round of coughing erupted. She turned away from the table.

"You okay?" Blaise asked, his voice concerned.

Hadley nodded, but the cough medicine should have lasted through dinner. Something was off...wrong. She felt worse than she had all week. Each breath hurt as if a belt was wrapped around her chest and someone kept pulling it tighter with each exhale.

The room swayed slightly.

Whoa.

What was happening?

Something clattered against a plate.

People stood.

A person shouted.

Everything was going dark, a fade-to-black camera effect taking over her vision.

Two hands held on to her.

"Hadley?" Blaise leaned into Hadley.

Or maybe she was the one against him. "I..."

"Hadley, it's Rizzo." The male voice was calm and steady, the exact opposite of her racing pulse and rapid breaths. "Remember me from the ride over? I want to check you, okay?"

She nodded.

Someone touched her forehead and then her cheek.

"She's burning up," Rizzo said. "She's also dehydrated."

"She wasn't this warm when I held her hand," Blaise said. "That was right after we arrived."

"Can you tell me what hurts, Hadley?" Rizzo asked.

"Chest. Hard to breathe. Cold." She forced out each word. "Tired. Need to sleep."

"I'll get the car," Rizzo said. "Take her outside through the emergency exit in the back. I'll pick you up in the alley."

Someone smoothed her hair. Must be Blaise.

She was too tired to open her eyes.

"Sorry," she mumbled.

"I'm the one who's sorry." Blaise's voice was thick. "You told me you didn't feel well, but I made us come."

"Let's get her up." That sounded like Adam.

"I'm carrying her," Blaise said. "I don't want to chance her falling."

"No." Her voice sounded raw. "I'm too heavy."

He picked her up. "You're perfect."

Yeah, right. Though Hadley hoped she remembered his words the next time she chose a donut over a piece of fruit. Because a donut would always win.

Blaise holding her brought much-needed warmth. She rested her head against his chest. The beat of his heart against her ear soothed her but didn't stop her eyes from stinging.

She was a professional. She had a plan. Getting sick wasn't part of that.

The next thing Hadley knew, she was sitting in the back of the SUV that Rizzo drove. Someone had buckled her seat belt. "What's going on?"

"You fell asleep." Blaise sat next to her, rubbing the top of her hand with his thumb. "We're going to the hospital."

She gave a shake of her head. *Oh, man.* Bad move. That hurt. "Too much trouble. I just need to sleep."

"You'll sleep soon." His voice comforted her, making it hard not to press into him, letting his warmth blanket her once again. "After a doctor examines you. I need to know what's going on."

"Me, too," Rizzo called from the front seat. "This is for the best."

Shadows flickered across Blaise's face, but they didn't hide his closed-mouth smile. He brushed her hair off her face. "You wouldn't want us to stay awake and worry all night."

"No." She didn't want that. "It's just a cold."

"Then this won't take long," he said softly. "And we'll be home soon."

Home.

And then she remembered.

She wasn't in San Francisco.

Hadley cringed. "I never checked in to the hotel."

"Don't worry." Blaise covered her hand with his. "I'll take care of it. Which hotel?"

It took her a minute to remember the name of the hotel and tell him. What was wrong with her brain?

"Hey." He cupped the side of her face with his hand. "It'll be okay."

She wished she felt as certain. "Thank you."

"For what?" he asked.

She coughed, the hacking sound much worse than it had been. "For being here. With me. It means…"

A lot.

* * *

"Pneumonia."

Hadley let the diagnosis sink into her exhausted brain. She was usually the definition of healthy, catching a cold or two each year but nothing else. She stared at the IV needle on the top of her hand where fluids were being pumped into her.

"You're sure?" Hadley assumed the doctor was telling her the truth, but she found it hard to believe a runny nose and sore throat could turn into pneumonia.

"Yes. It's what your friend Rizzo thought, and X-rays confirm it."

So it was true. She blew out a breath only to cough.

The doctor's gaze moved from her to Blaise, who stood in the corner of the ER treatment room. Rizzo had left thirty minutes ago, but she wasn't sure where he'd gone. She hoped he was sleeping. They'd been here all night.

"I don't have the blood test results," the doctor said. "The sputum culture won't come back for several days, but based on what I saw under the microscope, it's bacterial, not viral. I'll send you home with a prescription for antibiotics. You can use acetaminophen or ibuprofen for the fever. You also need to rest and stay hydrated. You should feel better shortly. If not, see your primary care physician. A full recovery can take weeks, even months."

That wasn't what she wanted to hear. "I live in San Francisco. I'm flying home Sunday. I mean, later today."

The doctor frowned. "You need to finish your antibiotics before you fly, and then see how you're doing before you get on a plane. You're young and healthy, but pneumonia is nothing to shrug off."

She coughed as if her body wanted to emphasize the point.

Blaise took a step toward the bed where she lay. "Hadley's not flying anywhere until she's recovered."

Easy for him to say.

She had responsibilities and obligations. Some could be done remotely, but not the meetings she had scheduled. She'd only booked one night at the hotel, using her reward points—those added up fast with her visits to New York—and she hoped they could extend her stay until she returned home.

"Stop thinking so hard," Blaise said. "You'll strain your brain."

Too late. Her mind was on total overload.

And that wasn't going to end.

Somehow she had to retrieve her car and suitcase from Blaise's house, find a pharmacy to fill her prescription, and check in to the hotel. A call to Fallon could wait until Hadley was settled in her room. She could text Ella tonight to ask what could be rescheduled. Working remotely wouldn't be the worst thing in the world though Hadley might need a day or two off until she could breathe better. But more time than that…

Hadley coughed again, wondering if she would hack up a lung before she felt better. Eyes burning, she blinked to keep the tears at bay. She couldn't lose it.

"Hadley?" Blaise asked.

She raised her chin, ignoring how the slight movement hurt. "Just a lot to figure out."

That was the safest thing she could say to him.

Hadley had to remain in control. Take things one step at a time. That was how she did everything—because it worked. Her recovery would be no different.

"Not for a few days." The dark circles under his eyes and his drawn face showed how tired he was. "You need to rest."

"So do you." Blaise had been with her except during the chest X-rays.

"After you finish the fluids, the nurse will be in to take out the IV and give you the discharge papers."

"Thanks," she and Blaise said in unison.

"Finish all your antibiotics even if you feel better. And don't overdo it." With that, the doctor left.

"I'm sorry." They spoke on top of each other again.

Blaise half laughed, but that didn't take away the weariness from his eyes. "You first."

"I'm sorry you had to be stuck here all night. You're losing your Sunday now." Breathing still hurt, but she continued on. "I'll be out of your hair—"

"Stop." His gaze hardened, reminding her of the rocks she and the kids had seen at Point Reyes. "You're coming home with me."

"But—"

He held up a hand. The tight lines around his mouth and deep creases on his forehead made her press her lips together. She'd never seen this side of him, but keeping quiet was probably a good idea.

"You heard what the doctor said. This isn't up for negotiation." His voice was steady and low. As he came closer, he never broke eye contact. "You need to rest. I have room at my house and people to make sure you do that."

People.

Something inside her shifted.

Blaise meant staff. Employees.

Whoever took care of his house.

He wouldn't be the one looking after her.

A steel band squeezed her chest tightly. The pneumonia, except she couldn't ignore the flash of disappointment.

Silly.

Blaise wasn't her boyfriend. He had a company to run. His priorities didn't include taking care of someone he'd hired. But he needed to keep up appearances for his friends. His "girlfriend" wouldn't stay in a hotel when he had a huge house.

"Th-thanks," she said.

"Let's get you feeling better, then we'll figure things out."

Not trusting her voice, she nodded.

Because she wasn't part of a "we," but for the first time in a long while, a part of her wished she was.

* * *

Adrenaline pounded through Blaise—the way it had since leaving the restaurant with Hadley. Memories of his times at the hospital with Wes, his mom, and his dad crashed into Blaise like an avalanche. Deep breaths hadn't helped calm the suffocating emotions, so he pinpointed his attention on Hadley, pushing everything else on his mind aside.

That had worked and got him through the long hours in the ER with her. Now that they were home and Hadley had barely eaten dinner after a nap, an impending dread of something else going wrong overtook him. He hadn't felt this way in years.

"You sure you don't want me to stick around," Rizzo said from the second floor landing.

A part of Blaise wanted to say yes, but his bodyguard had done so much already, including getting Hadley's prescription filled. "You've been up all night. When was the last time you slept? Thirty-six hours ago?"

"Lex is on tomorrow, so I plan to sleep my Monday away." Rizzo motioned to the closed door of Hadley's bedroom. "How are you doing?"

"I'm fine." Blaise fought the urge to yawn. He was tired, but he doubted he would sleep much or well. He may have ignored the memories, but they were still there, lurking inside him, waiting for their time to resurface. "If I need help tonight, I'll call you."

"Sounds good, boss." Rizzo glanced at the door again. "Get some sleep, too."

As Rizzo went downstairs, Blaise's phone buzzed. He didn't look at the screen. He'd received messages from everyone at the dinner, plus Wes, Dash, Brett, and Henry. Word had spread like wildfire. Blaise sent updates via their group text with a promise to message them again if there were any changes on Monday morning.

He eyed the guest bedroom's closed door. On the other side, Hadley was changing into her pajamas. He hated leaving her alone, even for a few minutes, but she hadn't wanted him to help her undress.

Yeah, he'd asked.

She'd said no.

It was taking her a long time. He knocked. "Hadley?"

"Almost finished." Two minutes later, the door opened. Her eyes remained glassy, but her face wasn't as flushed. "Sorry, I had to brush my teeth."

That didn't surprise him. She probably had a nighttime checkoff list so no task was forgotten. "No need to apologize."

She swayed and then leaned against the doorjamb.

His heart clenched, the way it had been doing since her collapse at the restaurant. He hated feeling so helpless, so useless. "Let's get you in bed."

A glass of water and a bottle of ibuprofen sat on the nightstand. Rizzo must have gotten those when he brought Hadley her medication.

She crawled beneath the covers in the queen-sized bed. "I appreciate your help. You must be exhausted."

"I'll be fine. There's one more thing I need to do before I turn out the lights."

She coughed before scrunching her nose. "What?"

He walked to her side of the bed. "I need to tuck you in."

As she gripped the edge of the comforter, her knuckles went white. "Why?"

"It's a Lowell family tradition, right?"

She stared warily, though some of the effect was lost because of her heavy eyelids, which kept wanting to close. "For the kids."

Blaise shrugged. "Audra and Ryder would approve."

Hadley coughed, sipped some water, and then placed the glass on the nightstand. "They would."

"So it's okay?" he asked.

Nodding, she lowered her gaze.

"I may be a newbie at tuck ins, but Audra and Ryder thought I did a decent job, so have faith."

That brought a chuckle.

What had Wes's medical team told him? Laughter was the best medicine, which had prompted comedy movie marathons and bad jokes galore. They hadn't stopped, either, once he went into remission.

Blaise pushed the edge of the sheet under the mattress. Strands of her auburn hair spread across the ivory pillowcase. He focused on doing his job. That appeared snug enough…

Memories rushed to the surface. His mother. His father. Putting them into bed. Cleaning up after them. Wondering if they were asleep or dead. Searching for a pulse or breath.

This is different.

Hadley will be okay.

Blaise repeated that.

It was true, but the old feeling of being out of his element was the same. So was his desire to help. Do what was right. Make her better.

As he double-checked the sheet, he tucked away his emotions. That was where they belonged, hidden not visible. "How's that?"

She smiled softly. "It's been years since someone tucked me in. You did a wonderful job."

His chest puffed. "Do I need to check for monsters?"

"No. I'm safe here."

She was kidding around, but pride swelled, knowing he'd done something right for her. Everyone needed to feel safe and secure. He would do what he could so she continued to feel that way with him.

"I'm leaving the door open," he said. "If you need anything, yell."

Her eyelids fluttered. She appeared to be losing the battle to keep them open.

"Sleep," he encouraged.

"Thanks again."

Her whisper-soft voice tugged on his heart. He would give anything to make her feel better. Maybe sleep coupled with the medication would be enough.

Hadley coughed before turning onto her side, but her eyes remained closed.

The woman lying in the bed was nothing like the strong, professional matchmaker he'd hired. This woman wasn't ruled by plans and her process. She was soft and vulnerable and needed someone.

Tonight, that person was him.

An unfamiliar yearning welled inside Blaise. He longed to hold her while she slept. That way if Hadley woke in the middle of the night, she would know she wasn't alone.

But he couldn't.

Instead, he turned off the lamp on the nightstand. The room went dark, but the hallway light allowed him to see. "Sleep well."

She didn't respond, but he hadn't expected her to.

Blaise brushed his lips over her forehead. Her skin wasn't as hot as it had been, but checking her temperature wasn't the reason for his kiss.

Now, she'd been tucked in completely.

He walked out of her room. At the doorway, he stopped and glanced over his shoulder.

Hadley intrigued him. She worked hard to give clients their happily ever after, but what about her?

Did she want one for herself?

Maybe she'd find one tonight while she slept. "Sweet dreams, princess."

Chapter Twelve

The next morning, Hadley didn't feel any better. The only bright spot was remembering how sweet Blaise had been when he'd tucked her in last night. The man continually surprised her, but more than that, he intrigued her. If he wasn't a client...

Except he was.

Which meant she couldn't think of him as anything other than someone who'd hired her.

She called Fallon and then Ella, speaking to them in between coughs. That wore her out so Hadley slept more, but it wasn't restful. She woke more tired than before.

A woman entered the bedroom, carrying a tray of food.

"Hi, I'm Robyn. Blaise's housekeeper."

She was in her fifties. A single braid of brown hair mixed with strands of gray fell to her mid-back. She wore black leggings, a coral tunic, and Birkenstocks. Mini dream catchers dangled from her earlobes. Crystals and charms hung from a thin leather cord around her neck.

Robyn placed the tray next to Hadley on the bed. "I have a bowl of chicken noodle soup."

"You didn't have to go to so much trouble for me."

"It's no trouble at all. The soup isn't homemade, because I'm a horrible cook. The chef will be here tomorrow. If you have any requests, please let me know."

Hadley found Robyn's honesty refreshing. Though if Blaise had another person cooking for him, he wouldn't need a housekeeper with those skills. "I appreciate you making me lunch, but I'm not that hungry."

"Not surprising because you're sick." With her easy smile and warm eyes, Robyn exuded the kindness and compassion of a nurturer. "Eat a few bites. You need your strength."

The woman's hypnotic voice soothed Hadley in an unexpected way. "I'll try." She swallowed a spoonful. "This is good."

"Blaise wants you to sleep as much as possible, so we'll get to know each other when you feel better," Robyn said. "Just push the tray over to the other side of the bed when you're finished. I'll pick it up later."

That sounded about all Hadley could manage at the moment. "Thanks."

Robyn glanced at the open suitcase sitting on the floor with clothes piled on top. "Blaise mentioned you were in New York last week. Most everything must be dirty. I'll wash your clothes."

Hadley sucked in a breath. A coughing fit erupted.

"I'll take your suitcase to the laundry room," Robyn said, without waiting for an answer. She picked up the luggage and clothes. "That will be easier and less distracting for you. Blaise is working from home today. I'm sure he'll be up to see you now that you're awake."

"O-kay," Hadley croaked.

Except it wasn't.

Not only was Robyn doing more work because of Hadley, Blaise had also stayed home when he should be at his office.

This was bad and shouldn't be happening.

She was used to taking care of herself. Fallon and the kids, too. Now someone else was having to do everything and she was in the way.

A lump burned at the back of Hadley's throat.

She ate another spoonful of soup, but it didn't make her feel better, so she pushed the tray to the empty side of the bed.

Stupid.

That was how she felt.

Stupid and tired and helpless.

A trifecta she'd never expected to be experiencing.

Least of all in Oregon.

Okay, she'd taken her medication, washed her face, and brushed her teeth this morning. But the trip to the bathroom had worn her out. Doing more...

Impossible.

Her chest ached. Each breath hurt. Tears burned.

She hated being sick.

She hated being stuck at Blaise's house.

She hated being a burden.

Her carefully planned life was spinning completely out of control. The worst part? Until the antibiotics started working, she couldn't do anything to make it better.

She hiccuped. Coughed. Cried.

As hot tears rolled down her face, she closed her eyes.

"Hadley?"

Her eyelids sprang open. She wiped her face.

Blaise stood in the doorway. He wore black pants and a white dress shirt unbuttoned at the neck. He rushed toward her and sat on the edge of the bed.

She must have missed a tear or two because he ran his finger down her cheek before lowering his arm. "What's wrong, sweetheart?"

His endearment felt like a caress. One that made

her sob.

"You hired me to do a job, and I'm sick." The words fell out. "I have to stay here and can't take care of myself. I can't do anything."

"You're sick." His voice remained steady. "That's not your fault."

"I haven't showered. I keep coughing. Now, I'm crying. This isn't like me at all. I'm a h-hot mess."

"No, you're perfect the way you are." He sounded sincere.

She glanced up at Blaise to find him staring at her. "Not perfect, but I do my best."

He smiled, the soft curve of his mouth made her wish she didn't look like one of the walking dead. Except she did, and if she were him, she'd fire herself and hire someone more professional.

Her shoulders drooped.

Feeling like a failure, she stared at the comforter.

"You go far beyond doing your best," he said.

She shook her head. "I'm supposed to have everything under control, but I haven't even opened my planner today or checked my email or—"

"You have pneumonia." He glanced at the other side of the bed. "Hang on a minute."

Blaise reached over her legs, picked up her lunch tray, and carried it to the dresser.

Feeling cold, she pulled up the comforter.

He returned to the bed. "Scoot over."

She did.

He sat next to Hadley, put his arm around her, and pulled her toward him. "This is better. Now, where were we?"

Playing space heater? His warmth surrounded her. She fought the urge to press against him, soak up his strength, cuddle.

She couldn't forget—client.

"I remember. Pneumonia," he said finally. "If you're this sick and able to work, then you'd be an anomaly. One we'd need to replicate."

She sighed, only to have to cough again. "I'm not used to feeling this way."

He studied her—his face pinching and his gaze intensifying. "You remind me of myself."

That was the last thing Hadley expected to hear. She stared at him through her eyelashes. "How?"

"You take care of people. Your sister. Your niece and nephew. Your assistant. Your clients."

"That's what you're supposed to do."

"Yes, but you can be a caretaker and still allow someone to take care of you, too." His earnest gaze matched his expression. "Wanting or needing help doesn't mean you failed or are weak. It only means you're human."

Hadley let his words sink in. Blaise didn't seem like a caretaker type, but... "Robyn takes care of you."

He nodded. "She does an excellent job as long as I keep her out of the kitchen."

That brought a laugh. "Robyn mentioned she wasn't much of a cook."

"She's beyond horrible. That's why I have a chef, too," Blaise explained. "When I was interviewing, I thought I'd hire one person to do everything, but once I met Robyn, I knew she was special. She didn't act or dress like the other applicants. The first thing she said to me during our interview was she smelled mold and, no matter who I hired, they needed to take care of it right away or I could suffer long-term health consequences."

"Was there mold?" Hadley asked.

"In the guest bathroom." He sounded amused.

"So are there other people in your life like Robyn?"

"Yes."

Hadley wanted to know more. "Who?

"Mr. Penney, a math teacher, and Coop, a custodian, from my high school."

"Good guys?"

Blaise nodded. "At times, I resented them, but I had no idea how desperately I needed them. My life was a hot mess, and they helped me. I wouldn't be where I am today without them."

The affection in Blaise's voice told Hadley how much those people meant to him, but he hadn't mentioned his parents. "What about your mom and dad?"

His muscles tightened, and his breath stilled. The

only movement, if she could call it that, was the rapid beating of his heart.

"Blaise?" she asked.

"I... It's..." He took a breath and then grimaced. "It's not a pretty story."

"Most real-life ones aren't." She leaned into his side, laying her arm across his chest. "I'd like to hear it if you wouldn't mind telling me."

He twirled the ends of her hair with his finger.

Physically she couldn't be any closer to him without scooting onto his lap, but his silence seemed to push them further apart.

"My parents were drug addicts." His voice cracked. "Heroin. It started when I was eight and went on for ten years."

His caretaker comment suddenly made sense. "You took care of them."

He nodded with a faraway, almost haunted, look in his eyes. "Thank goodness my mom had inherited my grandmother's house or we would have ended up homeless. As it was, there never was much food, but at least we had a place to call home. Though, when their sketchy friends came over to party, I took off for the night. Those people scared me."

Hadley tried to compare what his childhood must have been like to his life now. Tried and failed. "Where did you go?"

"Wherever they weren't." He half laughed.

The tortured sound made her cuddle closer. She

wanted to do something—anything—to comfort him.

"I begged them to go to rehab, but they said no. They didn't want to help themselves." Blaise took a breath and then blew it out. "I did what I could. Worked odd jobs until I was old enough to hold a regular one so we could buy groceries, but I had to keep the money hidden from them."

Hearing the resignation in his voice broke her heart. She hugged him. "They were lucky to have you as a son."

Blaise shrugged, but his expression was the opposite of indifferent. He tried to turn away from her, but she wouldn't let him. "They loved heroin more than they ever loved me."

The rawness of his words broke her heart. "Blaise…"

"It's the truth." His words were stilted yet dripped with emotion. His eyebrows squeezed together, a deep V forming above the bridge of his nose. "I didn't want to believe it then. But, I know that now."

"I wish you hadn't experienced that." She didn't know what else to say.

"Thank you." He pulled her so she was half on top of him. "Do you mind?"

Hadley didn't know if he needed the closeness or the warmth or to just know he wasn't alone. "It's fine. Nice."

And it was.

Despite the circumstances.

She rubbed her hand over his heart, not wanting to push him to tell her more, imagining a younger version of him when he'd had to take care of the two people who were supposed to care for and love him unconditionally.

Tears stung her eyes, but she blinked them away.

"My mom OD'd when I was seventeen. The same thing happened to my dad two weeks after my eighteenth birthday."

She gasped. "They're both—"

"Dead." The word reverberated through the room. "Heroin killed the people they'd once been long before their hearts stopped beating."

Hadley tightened her hold on him.

Blaise kissed the top of her head.

The sweet gesture melted her heart. He'd overcome overwhelming odds to succeed.

Incredible.

"The only blessing, if you want to call it that, was my age." He twirled her hair again. "I was old enough that foster care wasn't an option."

"But still…"

"It sucked," he said in a matter-of-fact tone. His gaze met hers. "You called yourself a hot mess, but you're not. Trust me, I know. I was one back then."

"You didn't let it stop you."

"I couldn't." He sniffled.

She touched his face, rubbing her palm against his

beard.

"The school's scholarship fund paid for an SAT test. I knew I'd only get one shot, so I aced it because college was my way out."

Pride and respect for Blaise quadrupled. "That doesn't surprise me."

"Mr. Penney helped me apply to college and found scholarships that I could qualify for. Coop helped me fix up the house so I could rent it while I was at school. He told me to sell it, but I couldn't. It was my only link to my parents, good or bad. I held on to it until I needed money to start Blai$e." He snickered. "A little bit ironic."

"No, smart," she countered. "You survived. Thrived. And look at what you've accomplished. Thank you for telling me."

"Only Mr. Penney, Coop, and an overpriced therapist know as much as you do."

Her mouth dropped open. "I won't say a word, but why haven't you told the guys? You're all so close."

Blaise's jaw jutted forward. His muscles bunched tighter. "I don't want their pity."

"Oh, Blaise." She embraced him once again. The man was brilliant, but he had it all wrong. Somehow, she needed to make him see that. "Pity is the last thing I feel for you. Try respect, admiration, awe. What you overcame is more impressive than the company you built. There's no reason to hide your

200

past."

He said nothing, but the way he blinked suggested he was considering what she'd said.

"Maybe I'll tell them." His eyes brightened. "After I win the bet."

That made her laugh. This man was dangerous in so many ways. Did he know that?

"Thanks for listening," he said.

"You had the hard part." Hadley expected him to let go of her, but he didn't. That brought more relief than it should, but she didn't care. She wanted this time with him. "Thank you for telling me."

"I should go."

"You need to work?"

"You need to sleep," he said a beat after her.

Hadley didn't want this closeness with him to end. "I could sleep nicely just like this."

Blaise hadn't loosened his hold on her. "Me, too."

She wanted to ask him to stay. She wanted to remain in his arms. She wanted to kiss him.

No kissing clients.

That was her rule.

One she wanted to break for the very first time.

Hadley coughed. That reminded her of another reason she couldn't kiss Blaise—pneumonia.

"Will you be back?" Hadley hated how breathless and desperate she sounded, but she couldn't help it.

"Of course." He let go of her so she moved off him. "So rest up. We can watch a movie."

Anticipation flowed through her. "Do you enjoy action-adventure or sci-fi?"

"I was thinking my matchmaker might enjoy a sweet rom-com."

Her heart swelled. "Oh, those are my favorites."

"I had a feeling they might be." He kissed her forehead before climbing off the bed. "See you soon."

Her skin tingled at the point of contact. Grinning, she wiggled her toes underneath the comforter. "I'm looking forward to it."

Chapter Thirteen

On Wednesday afternoon in his office, Blaise sat at his desk, trying to concentrate. He read the same paragraph twice, but he didn't remember one word. Not wanting to waste more time, he closed his laptop. He hated being distracted, which he'd been for days. Okay, since his trip to San Francisco over two weeks ago.

His knee bounced. His muscles twitched.

The rolling feeling in his stomach wouldn't stop.

This wasn't like him.

He needed to relax.

Closing his eyes, Blaise imagined the one person who might be able to settle him—Hadley. Picturing her, he inhaled, held his breath, and then exhaled. He repeated that two more times before opening his eyes.

A little better.

If only he were with her now.

He missed Hadley.

But he had one place to go before driving home.

Unfortunately.

He slumped in his chair, wishing the day were over. That it were Monday again, and he'd stopped himself from entering the guest bedroom to comfort...

No, he wouldn't change a thing with Hadley.

Cracking open his heart and spilling his soul to her had rocked Blaise to his core, but telling Hadley about his past had been the right move. He knew that with pulse-pounding certainty.

The way she'd held on to him had given Blaise strength to continue, to find more closure, something missing for too long. He couldn't change his past, but he also couldn't allow himself to be ashamed by what happened.

It wasn't his fault.

He knew—had known—that logically.

His parents hadn't been forced to try drugs. They'd chosen to take them. Not once, but over and over again. That choice had led to a disease—an addiction they couldn't beat.

Blaise had done what he could, as a kid and as a teenager, to help, but their answer to him had always been the same when he'd wanted them to get help.

I can't.

Except he'd heard something different all those years ago.

I can't because you're not worthy of my love.

I can't because you're not a good enough son.

I can't because you're not as important as the drugs.

After talking with Hadley the other night, however, his heart finally understood and embraced the truth. His parents had said *I can't*, but he was the one who had filled in the blanks back then. No longer.

Not. His. Fault.

The three simple words lifted the two-ton weight he hadn't realized he'd been carrying all these years. He had also learned something else.

He'd made a wrong decision, one that had been shadowing and mocking him for years. Keeping the past bottled up wasn't helping him. Refusing to share what happened with even his closest friends had fixed nothing. But telling Hadley…

Her easy acceptance, the way she'd praised him, gave him a sense of peace that had eluded him for too long.

After turning off her television and telling her goodnight later that Monday night, he'd stayed awake. He'd thought about her, his mom and his dad, and himself.

Maybe Blaise feeling like an outsider was his perception colored by his past, not reality. Maybe he should trust his friends with more of his story, not assume how they would react and reject him. Maybe he need to chill.

On Tuesday, Blaise had called his once-former high-priced therapist's office and made an appointment. Now he was freaking out. He could reschedule. People—patients—did that all the time.

Blaise considered it, but he wasn't stupid. Postponing would only delay the inevitable. He needed to go. He just hadn't imagined Dr. Alvarez adding an appointment slot so he could speak with Blaise.

Today.

In less than an hour.

He flexed his fingers to keep them from curling into fists.

His phone buzzed, a welcome relief from the silence. Maybe his appointment was being rescheduled.

Wishful thinking.

More like hopeful.

He grabbed his phone off the desk. Text messages filled the screen. None from Dr. Alvarez's office. One, however, caught Blaise's attention.

Robyn: *Hadley feels up to sitting in the family room so I'm making her a bed on the couch. Should I wait to serve her dinner or are you working late?*
Blaise: *Wait. I'll be home on time.*
Robyn: *Working from home on Monday. Now dinner at*

home for the second night in a row? Methinks Hadley is good for you.
Blaise: *Possibly.*
Robyn: *That means you agree. See you later.*

Did he agree?

Blaise scratched his neck. He enjoyed spending time with Hadley and wanted to get to know her better. His attraction to her grew each time they were together. Which had been a lot this week. But the feelings went deeper than the physical. That was unexpected. He'd like to claim unwelcome, but he wasn't sure because he couldn't remember the last time he'd felt so close to anyone as he did with Hadley.

Not that how he felt mattered.

He'd hired her.

To win the bet, not to fall in love himself.

Wait.

Love wasn't an option. It wasn't on the table.

He scrubbed his hands over his face.

She worked for him. They'd become friends.

Yeah, friends.

Nothing else.

"Blaise," Trevor said from the doorway. His crooked tie and tired eyes suggested the guy must still be having issues with the database system. "You mentioned leaving at three thirty. It's almost time."

"Thanks for the reminder." As Blaise packed his

laptop in his bag, he noticed Trevor lean against the doorjamb. "Take the rest of the afternoon off."

Trevor's eyes widened. "Really?"

His disbelief in that one word shocked Blaise. Was he that demanding a boss? He remembered what a board member had told him about the difference between honey versus vinegar leadership styles. Blaise used the latter, but he was willing to experiment with the other. "Yes."

Trevor straightened, relief pouring from him. "I, uh, thank you. Enjoy the rest of your day."

"You, too." Blaise left the office, more in a hurry than he should be, given where he was going. But the sooner he spoke to Dr. Alvarez, the sooner Blaise could go home.

He wanted to be there already.

A delicious dinner to fill his stomach, a silly movie to make him laugh, and his friend, Hadley, to keep him company.

It would be another good night. He had a feeling he might need it.

* * *

Hours later, after surviving the appointment and making another for next week, Blaise sat on the couch next to Hadley. Covered by a throw, she leaned against a pillow. He would have preferred her resting on him in her bed like the past two nights where they'd watched movies.

But this was less intimate with a bowl of popcorn, a cup of hot herbal tea for her, and a bottle of beer for him.

A good idea under the circumstances. Even if his arm wanted to slip around her and pull her close.

Another rom-com flick played on the television. Earlier, they'd eaten dinner in these exact spots. His choice because he didn't want her to get tired. A good decision because she'd been yawning. Still, that didn't stop her smile from lighting up her face.

Not because of anything he'd done.

No, this had to do with the movie. She loved romantic chick flicks so much.

Even though the movie continued to play, he ignored the screen and watched her. The expressions crossing her face were as entertaining as the film. Maybe more so.

She laughed.

The sound sent a burst of warmth shooting from him. "You're enjoying this one."

Hadley nodded. "It's one of my favorites. The actors have great chemistry. And it's such a sweet story."

The other two movies had been "sweet," too. She obviously had a type she preferred. One that he shouldn't find too surprising given what he knew about her. But that made him wonder why she was still single.

"You're a romantic at heart. You're a skilled matchmaker," he said. "Why aren't you dating anyone?"

Her gaze traveled from the television to him. "Don't you want to finish the movie?"

He would have expected to be talked out after his appointment, but Dr. Alvarez's questions brought out others. Ones for Blaise to answer eventually and some he wanted to ask Hadley.

"Let's take a break." He paused the movie. "Need more tea?"

Angling her shoulders toward him, she raised her mug. "I have enough."

"Hungry?"

"Not after that dinner." She touched her stomach. "The lasagna was to die for."

"The tiramisu is waiting for us in the refrigerator."

"And we'll get to it, but I need a break first or I'll explode."

"So, dating?" he asked.

"I thought you might have forgotten the question."

"Never."

She took a sip. "I've had little luck with relationships, so I took a break from dating and it keeps getting extended."

"Why?" He studied her. She wore no makeup. Her complexion was still pale, but her cheeks had a rosy color to them. Her hair was tangled. "You're smart and beautiful. Kind. And compassionate."

Gratitude flared in her eyes. Hadley stared over the lip of her mug. "Please, go on."

Blaise laughed. "I'm serious."

"So am I."

Except he could hear the humor in her voice. "Does living in San Francisco make dating harder? Or is it your family?"

"It's a few things." She stared at the fireplace, but her gaze was unfocused. "I may possess a gift for finding the perfect spouses for clients, but I've had zero luck myself. I've tried, but I fell for men who weren't...transparent."

"What happened?" Curiosity removed any hesitation he may have had asking.

Turning her attention to him, Hadley raised a brow. "You want the gory details?"

Yes. He'd take names, too. But admitting that might be rude. "How about you give me the condensed version?"

She took a breath and then blew it out. "They...used me."

His hands clenched. "They?"

"I wish it had been just one." Hadley half laughed. "You think someone cares about you the same way you do about them, but all they really want is something from you. It...hurts."

Her words hit like a left hook. Blaise's muscles

bunched. He forced himself to breathe. "I want something from you."

"Not like them." She touched the top of his hand as if to emphasize the point. "You hired me to do a job. I know what you want, and I'm being highly compensated," she explained in a calm voice. "It's a fair and even exchange, a business transaction."

Good, because the thought of hurting her slayed him. "Thanks for clarifying that."

"No problem."

She kept her hand on him, and he enjoyed her touch. That was something he'd missed last night—the contact with her.

Amusement twinkled in her eyes. "Now if you wanted me to do your homework so you could play football. Or were trying to steal my work and promotion while saying how much you loved me. Or wanted me to make another woman jealous while asking if I wanted to spend the holidays with you, then it would be another story."

Losers. They didn't deserve Hadley. "I'm sorry they hurt you."

She appeared resigned, not upset. "It's that adage about kissing frogs. I just wasn't ready to kiss more after that."

What about now? Blaise's fingernails dug into his palms. He didn't like thinking about her kissing anyone past, present, or future that wasn't him.

He needed to change the subject. "Does it bother

you that the guy in the movie is using his boss to get what he wants?"

Hadley shot Blaise a sideward glance. "He's not using her."

The serious expression on her face, the way her lower lip stuck out, and her matter-of-fact tone was adorable. She would hate him using that adjective, but it was true.

"His boss wants to stay in the country," Hadley continued. "He wants to be an editor. Nothing's secret or hidden."

"They're transparent."

"Exactly." She set her tea on the coffee table. "And that's what I'll look for when I date again."

When, not if.

Interesting.

"I mean, someday. Family and business are my priorities. I have little spare time."

"Same." He liked how they could talk so easily about things. "It's why I date, but only casually. Zero time for anything more."

"Any ex-girlfriends?" If she was trying to hide her curiosity, she was failing.

He forced himself not to smile. "No."

"But you're rich and handsome." Her befuddled tone was cute, and her compliment made him sit taller.

"I wasn't always rich," he joked.

She laughed. "But you've always been

handsome."

"Not even close," he admitted. "In school, students knew me as the malnourished nerd. I'm sure I was number one on the school's undatable list."

Her lips parted. "They had one?"

"Well, if there'd been one, I'd have been in the top position. In college, I worked two jobs, so there wasn't time for anything else. And now, I'm still busy."

"So it's work keeping you from dating, not your…past?" Hadley asked.

She meant his parents. Dr. Alvarez had brought up something similar during their session, but that was his job. However Hadley… "If the matchmaking doesn't work out, I see a future for you in counseling."

Her face scrunched. "Huh?"

"I visited my old therapist today."

Smiling, she leaned toward Blaise, her hand squeezing his. "How did it go?"

He forced himself not to lace his fingers with hers. "Not as bad as I thought it would be. I'm going back next week."

"It's so great you made that call."

Satisfaction flowed through him. "Opening up to you was the first step."

"And there will be many more." Happiness radiated from her, making him want to soak it up. "But don't forget. When you're ready to date or if you meet someone, don't come up with excuses so you can't have a relationship. You own the company. Find the time."

Her entire demeanor shifted because she'd put on her matchmaker hat, which told him two things—she was feeling better, and he'd been spending time with the real Hadley, not the one she showed to clients. The realization shouldn't have pleased him as much as it did.

"You've been doing that this week. Working from home. Leaving early enough to have dinner with me," she added. "That means you have some flexibility."

Yes, but he hadn't thought about taking advantage of that until her. Which was why he shrugged off what she said. "What kind of host would I be if I worked all day and went out to dinner as I usually do while you're here?"

"Robyn's around."

Blaise wasn't sure what she was getting at. "Would you rather I hadn't come home tonight?"

"No." The word rushed out. Hadley's cheeks turned pink, but this time, he wasn't worried about her having a fever. "That's not what I meant. I enjoy our evenings together."

Good.

"Me, too." Truth was, he would miss her when she returned to San Francisco. But that wasn't something he wanted to think about tonight. "Want to finish the movie?"

"Yes, please." She faced the television screen. "I'm ready for the HEA."

"HEA?" he asked, unfamiliar with the term.

"Happily ever after."

Of course. That must be why she enjoyed these movies so much.

"If anyone deserves a HEA, you do." He pressed play, wondering if she would laugh, cry, or sigh when this one finished.

Knowing Hadley, maybe all three.

* * *

On Friday night, Blaise sat with his friends in Dash's over-the-top backyard. Lights were strung across the extravagant patio, which contained a fully stocked bar with four beer taps, a gourmet outdoor kitchen, firepit, and a barbeque grill on steroids.

Typical Dash.

Blaise had come over after having dinner with Hadley. She was at his house. Cambria, Selah, and Rachael had stayed home. He'd only wanted the six of them here tonight. Henry and Brett hadn't been invited. Blaise would talk to them, but first, he needed to see how Adam, Dash, Kieran, Mason, and Wes reacted.

Iris had put out chips and salsa on the table. Some homemade guacamole and spinach-artichoke dip, too. That went better with the beer and whiskey they were drinking than cookies and brownies, though those were in the kitchen. But she wasn't here, either. Lights twinkled in the charming guesthouse off to the left in the backyard where she lived.

Sitting with friends, eating and drinking, was a great end to the week. If only that was the reason they were there.

A lump returned to Blaise's throat. It didn't burn as hot as it had with Hadley. Progress? He hoped so.

"So what did you want to talk about?" Dash asked him.

"Don't tell me," Mason teased. "You and Hadley are engaged."

"Give them another month or two." Kieran raised his beer in a mock toast. "Not everyone falls in love overnight like you."

As jokes about dating and fast engagements went around the table, Blaise sipped his stout.

Okay, he was procrastinating. So sue him.

"There's something I want…need to tell you." He blew out a breath, trying to ignore the hammering of his heart. "I've been vague about my parents, but there's a reason. They were heroin addicts."

No one said a word. No one moved. No one even blinked.

He continued talking, the words spilling out. He didn't look at anyone. Not because he needed to concentrate. No, this was fear—plain and simple. So, he'd focused on the salsa that had dropped on the table. The only other thing he did was keep flexing his fingers. He wasn't sure why, but it helped him.

When he'd told them everything, he forced himself to glance around the table.

His friends stared at him with expressions ranging from disbelief to confusion.

Except for Wes. His nostrils flared. His narrowed lips matched his hard gaze.

That was unexpected.

And disappointing.

Blaise fought the urge to stand up and ask Wes what he was thinking because Blaise had thought—believed—Wes would understand, more so than anyone else.

Wrong.

That cut deep.

Blaise had screwed up. Wes's response was proof of that. Blaise only hoped he could repair the damage.

"That's everything." He took another sip, gripping his glass like a lifeline, which probably was worrying his friends, so he loosened his hold and set the pint on the table. "I'm sorry for not telling you before. I… I wasn't ready."

"Dude." Dash refilled Blaise's glass. "Don't apologize. What you went through sucks. Big-time. I'm just glad you feel comfortable telling us now. You mentioned a few things over the years, but none of us took the time to dig deeper. That's on us, not you. I'm sorry for not being a better friend."

Blaise's jaw dropped. His ears rang. He couldn't believe what Dash was saying. But he was relieved and thankful, oh so thankful, for having a friend like him.

"Out of the mouth of babes," Adam murmured.

Kieran nodded. "Leave it to the Wonderkid."

The others nodded except for Wes, whose eyes were dark and serious.

"I don't get it." Wes sounded confused and angry, annoyed and frustrated, too. "All those times at the hospital, hour after hour during my treatments, and you never thought to tell me about your parents."

"Easy, big guy," Mason cautioned.

"It's okay," Blaise said. Whatever Wes was feeling had to come out, too. "Go on, Wes."

"That your mom and dad OD'd, and you found each of them." Wes's voice was strained. "You didn't think we needed to know that in case you had an anxiety attack or PTSD or something?"

Shaking his head, Mason covered his mouth with his hand as if to keep himself from saying something he shouldn't.

Adam rubbed the back of his neck.

Kieran blew out a breath. "Wes…"

"Some bad memories surfaced when I was at the hospital with you. I dealt with them." Blaise had never lied to anyone. He'd just withheld some facts. "I wanted to be with you."

"You were going through chemo," Adam reminded Wes as if he could have forgotten. "Blaise wasn't ready to discuss his parents. Even if he had been, he was there for your appointment. For you. And he didn't lose it. He held himself together, which you should be proud of. I am."

Adam's words gave Blaise a much-needed boost. The way what Dash said had.

A vein throbbed at Wes's jaw. Lines formed around his mouth. "What makes tonight the right time?"

Mason cursed. "Stop being such a—"

"Don't." Kieran patted Mason's shoulder.

Mason pressed his lips together.

"It's a valid question." Blaise wanted nothing to come between the six of them. These men were the closest thing he had to family—brothers. The only ones who could understand the wild ride he'd been on with Blai$e. He didn't want to lose that. Or them. "Hadley said I should tell you."

Wes's posture went ramrod stiff. "She knows?"

"She knows." Hadley had described their relationship as a business transaction, but this week they'd become closer. No kissing, but their touches and glances made him want...more. If only she could stay in Portland, but she would fly home on Sunday. "I'd been keeping the past hidden, locked away deep inside me, pretending what happened didn't matter. That was a mistake. One I didn't realize until I told her."

"I'm happy you did," Adam said.

The others nodded.

"So you like her?" Wes asked, his tone more neutral.

"I like her." How much, Blaise wasn't ready to admit, not even to himself.

Dash laughed, his smile growing. "You know, when I found out she was a matchmaker, I thought you'd hired her so you could win the bet. Looks like I was wrong."

"The same thing crossed my mind after I ran a search on her." The smile tugging on Wes's lips brought a rush of relief to Blaise.

Which was why he couldn't lie to them.

"The bet has come up," he said.

"I mentioned it to Hadley at the restaurant on Saturday night," Mason admitted.

"Of course you did." Wes snorted. "Misery loves company."

Kieran laughed. "We'd be miserable without our lovely wives."

Mason raised his glass of whiskey. "We want you three to be as happy as we are, and if Blaise's matchmaker can help with that…"

Wes rolled his eyes the way he always did. "Be

honest, you want to split the fund six ways. Which is what will happen if Dash, Blaise, and I marry in the next nine months."

Blaise decided keeping quiet was the smartest move.

Mason shrugged half-heartedly. "Who wouldn't want to split the money?"

"The last single man standing." Smiling, Dash leaned over the table. "Is Hadley going to find women for Wes and me to go out with?"

Wait? The guy sounded excited. Was Dash willing to go along with Blaise's plan? That would make things easier when Hadley found potential matches to introduce to the guys. He didn't want her worrying about making a mistake. "I'm sure she could. Are you game?"

"As long as I don't have to do anything other than pay for the date, sure," Dash said. "You know me."

"Mr. Status Quo, hates change, don't make me be social," they all said in unison.

"I'll drink to that." Dash took a sip of his beer.

Tonight was not turning out as Blaise imagined. He'd built this up in his head, but only Wes had any issues, and those seemed to come more from concern about Blaise. His friends were the best. "I'll mention it to her."

"What about you, Wes?" Kieran asked. "Do you

want Hadley to find you a date?"

Wes shrugged. "It's been a while."

"Annabelle?" Mason asked. Of course he would be the one to say the name of the woman who was never mentioned around Wes.

Wes nodded before sipping his club soda.

Tension hung in the air, thick like the smoke from the Eagle Creek Fire in the Columbia River Gorge two years ago. Annabelle Noble was *persona non grata*. She'd broken up with Wes after his cancer diagnosis and moved to the East Coast, much to everyone's relief.

Wes needed a woman in his life who cared about him, who wouldn't be afraid of cancer, and who didn't care about his money.

"Are you interested in going on a date?" Blaise asked, but he wanted to give Wes an out. "If not, no worries."

"I guess I'd be up for meeting someone new." Wes's expression was unreadable. His tone steady and unemotional. "But one date is all I'm committing to. One."

Blaise sat dumbfounded. This was almost too easy. Nothing had ever been easy for him. He wasn't like the others, who'd had normal parents.

"One date is fine," he said.

Because knowing Hadley, she would know exactly who fit perfectly with Wes. They didn't call her the wife finder for nothing.

Blaise bit back a grin. He'd told his friends the truth about his past, and four accepted him. Wes was coming around. Blaise could be patient. He would focus on winning the bet.

Who would fall first? Wes or Dash?

Blaise raised his glass. He couldn't wait to find out.

Chapter Fourteen

Saturday morning, Hadley woke to weak daylight filtering around the edges of the blinds. Rain pounded against the roof. Another wet and gray day in the Pacific Northwest, but she didn't mind. All the lush, green plants and trees made up for the wetness. Besides, she didn't have to go outside.

Not today.

She glanced at the clock.

9:28 AM.

That was later than she thought.

Though she wasn't surprised she'd slept in.

Last night, Hadley had tried to stay awake until Blaise arrived home. She must have fallen asleep. Even though she had wanted to see him, that was a good thing. Rest was what she needed to continue to recover.

After a quick shower, she pulled on a pair of black leggings, a teal sweater, and pink, fuzzy llama slipper socks Audra had given Hadley for her birthday.

Thinking of her niece sent a swell of emotion through Hadley. She missed Audra, Ryder, and Fallon—Tiny, too—but tomorrow, she would be home.

Home.

She shimmied her shoulders in anticipation. Sure, they'd kept in touch via phone calls and video chats, but she couldn't wait to be with them again. The noise, the mess, the chaos.

The hugs.

Hadley, however, would miss being with Blaise. This week with him had been not only surprising but also...

Special.

A ball of heat settled at the center of her chest. Who would have thought quiet evenings eating, watching movies, and talking with the same person could be so enjoyable? Especially when that person was Blaise Mortenson.

She would miss that.

Him.

He'd done so much for her since she'd been sick, but it was more than that. Something else was happening. Something she didn't want to define. She couldn't.

Hadley worked for him. He'd hired her so he could win the bet.

But this past week, they'd become friends.

Yes, friends.

A friend she was attracted to, dreamed about, and wanted to kiss again.

She hadn't done the last thing.

And wouldn't.

Because that was against her rules.

Ready to hear how last night with his friends had gone for Blaise, Hadley made her way downstairs and entered the kitchen. Someone sat at the island. Dash.

With a bright smile on his face, he raised his coffee mug. "Good morning."

Hadley glanced around. No one else was there. "Where's Blaise?"

"In his office on a conference call." Dash motioned to a pink box decorated with black lettering and characters. "I brought donuts. Help yourself."

Her mouth watered. Coffee no longer tempted her. She'd developed a taste for herbal tea and honey thanks to Robyn, but she hadn't eaten a donut in forever. Okay, a week and a half. That was long enough.

"Thanks." She filled a glass with water, sat on the stool next to Dash, and grabbed a maple bar with two slices of bacon on top. That counted as protein, right? She took a bite. "Delicious."

"Thanks for telling Blaise to talk to us last night. It wasn't easy for him, but it went well. And his past is something we need to know about him." Dash sipped his coffee. "Now we can help him. If he needs it. Because that's what friends do."

"Yes, it is." Dash was too cute, and whatever went down last night sounded good. That made her happy. "You guys are lucky to have each other."

"We are. And I know they don't only want to hang with me because of my money." Dash laughed. "Though let's be real. I'm more like the annoying kid brother the others tolerate."

Dashiell Cabot was the youngest of the six. He was also an interesting combination of genius and gamer. When they'd watched the football game, he'd bounced from one subject to another, the same way a dog might find his attention all over the place in a forest full of flying squirrels. Today he appeared more focused. Maybe he did better one-on-one.

She picked up her maple bar. "Every group needs one of those."

His mouth slanted in a charming, lopsided smile. "Yeah, and now they're stuck with me. They couldn't get rid of me if they tried."

She laughed. "Have they?"

Mischief gleamed in his eyes. "Possibly."

"But you're still here."

"I am." He opened the lid to the donut box but let it drop. "Last night, Blaise mentioned something about you finding me and Wes dates."

What? Hadley tried to keep her features neutral. She had no idea what was going on, but she would go with it. "I haven't spoken with Blaise since he went over to your house. I was asleep when he got home, but I'd be happy to find dates for you and Wes."

Hadley purposely said *dates* because saying *wives* might not go over well, even though she'd been hired to find them. She ate another bite of her donut. So tasty.

Dash drank more coffee before pushing a few sheets of paper toward her. "Blaise asked me to fill this out. I emailed an electronic version to you, but here's a print copy, too."

"Thanks." She appreciated his thoughtfulness because she was old school about some things. A glance told her he'd completed her questionnaire. "This will help me."

"Blaise said you might have some questions."

"A few."

Dash turned his coffee cup a quarter one way and then back again. "That should be okay."

He sounded uncertain. That wasn't good. "Do you want to go out with someone?"

"Sure," he blurted. "I mean, probably not if I had to go out and meet someone, text back and forth a bunch of times, and then make a date happen on my own. That's too much work, you know?"

She nodded, trying not to smile.

"But Blaise and you are together. He says you're good at your job. I looked you up to confirm it."

"It's smart to know what you're agreeing to."

It was Dash's turn to nod. "Blaise is so happy when he talks about you, and it's cool you're a matchmaker. So, I want to do this for him. And maybe I'll get something out of it for me."

The guy was super-sweet to want to go on a date to make Blaise happy. "My job is to make sure *you* get something out of it."

"Okay."

As she read his questionnaire, she ate more of the donut. "Would you mind answering a few questions now? That will help me narrow down your wants and needs for a future partner."

"Future date." He winked. "They might call you the wife finder, but let's not go crazy here."

Oops. She laughed. That had been her mistake. A good thing she hadn't mentioned finding him *the one*.

"I know what I want," he continued. "I want to meet a woman who has her own interests so she won't get bored when I'm working and who doesn't hate video games since I love playing them."

Simple needs, but Hadley needed to know more. "That's helpful. Now let's see if we can drill down a bit."

An hour later, Dash had answered her questions, peppered her with ones of his own, and eaten two more donuts.

"So, what happens next?" he asked.

"I'll fill in your file and start my search." Hadley had a better picture of Dashiell Cabot, Wonderkid of Silicon Forest, and what kind of woman would fit best with his personality and lifestyle. "When I find a match or two, I'll be in touch."

Dash stood. "Sounds good. I have a meeting, so I'm leaving. Tell Blaise bye."

These guys worked seven days a week, but then again, sometimes she did, too. "I will. Have a nice day."

Hadley made herself a cup of tea and placed Dash's mug in the dishwasher. The pink box on the island kept taunting her. Finally, after wiping off the countertops, she gave in and removed a cake donut with white icing and multicolored candy sprinkles.

"What's better than one donut?" she asked herself aloud. "Two!"

She took a bite.

"Taste good?" Blaise entered the kitchen and family room area.

"Yes."

He carried a coffee cup—an empty one based on the way he held it. He wore track pants and an old T-shirt that had seen better days, but he looked gorgeous.

Oops. Time to focus on something available to her.

She motioned to the box. "Lucky for you, Dash

and I didn't eat all of them."

"Thanks, but I had one before my call." Blaise refilled his cup before joining her at the island. "Did you talk to Dash?"

"I did." She glanced at the paperwork sitting on the island. "He filled out the questionnaire and answered my questions. Does this mean last night with your friends went well?"

A slow smile spread, crinkling the corners of his eyes and making her want to reach for her phone to capture his expression with a photograph. "It went better than I ever expected."

She touched his arm but then pulled her hand away when she realized what she'd done. "I'm so happy for you."

"Thanks. Me, too." Blaise took a sip of coffee. "Wes was the only one who seemed upset, which surprised me, but it'll be okay. Things were better by the end of the night."

"Yay!"

"Yes, yay." Blaise told her what had happened. "When the bet came up, I told everyone you and I had discussed it. I didn't want to lie, and then Mason chimed in. And…"

"Now I have permission from Dash and Wes to set them up on dates," she finished for Blaise.

He nodded. "Dash offered to come by this morning. But Wes is spending the rest of the weekend at his place in Hood Hamlet. You won't get to talk to him this weekend."

"I'll figure out a way to talk to him before you go home."

Blaise rubbed his chin. "But you'll be in San Francisco."

"I know."

His lips parted. "Does this mean you're thinking about making an exception to your rules?"

"I am." Which wasn't like her, but this wasn't a typical situation, either. She wanted this to work for Blaise and his friends, even if it meant changing how she did things.

"Thank you."

Two simple words, but the emotion behind them took her breath away. She swallowed. "You're welcome."

He sipped his coffee. She finished her donut. The silence wasn't uncomfortable. They didn't need to fill the quiet with meaningless words. Being in the same space as Blaise was enough.

Finally, he stood and refilled his cup. "So, what do you want to do on your last day in Portland?"

* * *

That evening, as the movie credits rolled, Blaise sat next to Hadley on the couch. A blanket covered them. A fire crackled in the fireplace. A bowl of popcorn, boxes of movie candy, and drinks sat on the coffee table.

If this had been a date, it would be one of the best. But it wasn't a date. Something he had to keep reminding himself. "Thanks for wanting to watch my favorite movie series today."

Hadley smiled at him. "I've never seen the *Harry Potter* movies all in a row like this."

"Movie marathons are great, but it's been a while since I've had time to do it." Years, actually. This week with Hadley, he'd watched more television than during the first eight months of the year. Not that he minded.

"It's fun." She grabbed a piece of licorice from one of the candy boxes he'd found in the pantry. "Did you read the books?"

"I love them." A fourteen-year-old Blaise had discovered a way to transport himself to another place—a safer place—when he cracked open that first book in the series. He'd read all night long. As soon as he'd reached the end, he started over. "I checked out the books from the library and read them as many times as I could before they were due."

"Is Harry your favorite?" she asked.

"Who wouldn't want to find out they were a wizard and their life was going to be completely different?" The words vomited out of him. Blaise couldn't stop because the books had been his escape. "I mean…"

Hadley pressed her shoulder against his, her

softness and warmth an appealing combination. "You related to Harry."

Blaise's face warmed. "In my daydreams."

"And real life," she said to his surprise. "Harry used a wand and magic, but you had something equally powerful to help you create a different life from the one you knew."

His heart rate kicked up a notch. "What?"

"Your brain. Not to mention your determination."

Her comparison touched him. "A wand and magic would have been cooler."

She laughed. "True, but you used what you had."

Their legs touched underneath the blanket they shared but nothing more. He kept himself from scooting closer. The accidental brush of their hands reaching for popcorn was enough. At least that was what he told himself because it had to be. Hadley was too tempting, and he didn't want to do anything stupid.

Tomorrow, she'd be home, and he'd be…

Nope.

Blaise wouldn't think about it. The next movie began. "When you were younger, did you ever want to find out you were a wizard?"

"No." Her blue eyes danced. "But I dreamed about being the long-lost princess from some faraway, exotic country. I devoured the *Princess Diaries* books, and I can't wait to share the series with Audra once she's old enough."

"I shouldn't be surprised since you enjoy"—Blaise searched for the term Hadley had used before—"HEAs."

"Yes, and I also love tiaras," she teased.

Now that surprised him. He studied her. "I'm trying to picture you in one, but a tiara doesn't quite fit with the fastidious matchmaker I've come to know."

She shrugged but was smiling. "I don't have much opportunity to wear mine, but sometimes a girl needs to put on her tiara and dance around. You can forget your troubles and just enjoy yourself."

He would pay money to see that. "Do you do that?"

"I have once or twice." She didn't hesitate answering. Again, that was something he would love to see.

"Do you have a wand?" Hadley asked.

His cheeks heated. "Yes, I have a…collection of them."

Hadley's face brightened. "Can I see them?"

"They're on display at an exhibit."

Her eyes widened. "Must be some collection."

"It was one of my first splurges after Blai$e was doing well." Buying signed, first edition hardcovers of the entire series was another.

"Have you ever waved a wand to see if you could influence the stock market?"

That made him laugh. "No, but there have been times I should have tried that."

"Couldn't hurt."

No, and that might have made him feel better. "Do you have your tiara with you?"

"Alas, I do not. I've never considered traveling with mine." She tilted her head. "Though now that you've mentioned it, I might have to add that to my packing list. Given how well I was cared for this week by you and Robyn, a tiara would be appropriate since I've been fêted like a princess."

He wasn't surprised she had a packing list, but hearing her say she was treated like a princess made his chest thrust out. "Next time, remember the tiara."

She bit her lip. "The movie's on."

Hadley focused on the television, but the light in her eyes had dimmed. And Blaise knew why.

There wouldn't be a next time for them.

Even if he wished there could be.

* * *

"Door-to-door service." Hadley sat next to Blaise in the back of the black SUV driven by Lex. Rizzo rode shotgun. "I could have flown commercial. Alone."

"No," all three men said in unison.

"I have a dinner in Palo Alto tonight," Blaise said without missing a beat. "Making a quick detour to the Marina District is no trouble."

Lex double-parked in front of her condo building. "And you're home."

Hadley was excited to see her family, but a part of her was missing Blaise, even though he was seated beside her. She may have been sick, but she enjoyed being with him. It didn't matter that they'd been homebodies. She preferred that to going out. And last night watching his favorite movies had been...perfect.

She wouldn't have changed anything. Well, except if he would have kissed her goodnight after they'd walked upstairs.

Hadley cleared her throat. "Thanks."

"I'll get the suitcase." Rizzo hopped out of the vehicle.

Blaise unbuckled his seat belt. "Let's get you inside. The kids must miss their aunt Hadley."

A few minutes later, she stood at her front door.

"Take care of yourself, Hadley. It could be weeks before you feel one hundred percent. Don't overdo it." Rizzo let go of the suitcase. "I'll be in the car with Lex, boss."

"Thanks," Blaise said.

All Hadley had to do was turn the doorknob and walk inside, yet she hesitated. This was her home. But Blaise...

"Did you forget your key?" he asked.

Pull yourself together.

She did, opened the door, and stepped inside. The familiar scents in the air made her take a deep breath.

"I'm home."

Screams filled the condo. Audra, Ryder, and Tiny came running toward her. Hadley hugged each one as the kids talked over each other to tell her all she'd missed. Tiny wove a figure-eight pattern between her legs.

"Welcome home." Fallon came out of the kitchen. She extended her right arm to Blaise. "I'm Fallon Caples."

He shook her hand. "Blaise Mortenson."

Fallon smiled. "So, you're the infamous Mr. M I've been hearing about, and the reason I must go into the closet each night."

"Sorry, not sorry," Blaise joked.

Audra and Ryder giggled.

"See, Mommy," Audra said. "We told you he was nice."

"You did." Fallon's gaze zeroed in on Hadley. "You're pale."

Hadley had a feeling Fallon would go all mom on her. "I'm getting over pneumonia. It takes a while to fully recover."

"She's been following the doctor's orders," Blaise said.

"Glad to hear that." Fallon sounded amused because she knew Hadley was a rule follower and would do what the doctor said. "Are you staying for dinner, Blaise?"

The kids jumped up and down with shouts of

"please."

"Thanks for the invite, but I can't," he said. "I have an event to attend. I need to get going."

The kids' faces dropped.

Ryder's lower lip stuck out. "But you just got here."

"I'm sorry," Blaise said, sounding sincere.

Hadley worked hard to keep her smile in place even if she understood their reaction. She didn't want to say goodbye to Blaise, either. Now that she was in direct contact with Dash and Wes—who was calling her tomorrow—she had no reason to stay in touch with Blaise. The next time she spoke to him would be to tell him she'd found matches for his friends.

The realization sucked the air out of her lungs.

Fallon's gaze bounced between Hadley and Blaise. "Kids, why don't you take your aunt's suitcase and purse to the bedroom, so she can say goodbye to Mr. M. I need to check on dinner."

Less than thirty seconds later, Hadley stood alone in the living room with Blaise. Three feet separated them, but the distance felt as if it were twenty times that. Where once the silence between them was comfortable, now awkwardness laced the quiet.

She hated it. Hated this. "Thanks for everything."

"Anytime, but you did more for me than I did for you."

Confused, she crinkled her nose. "Huh?"

"Getting me to open up, acting like my girlfriend

in front of my friends, making me realize I spend too much time working and need more balance in my life."

Hadley let what his words soak in. "You're welcome, but this was an even exchange."

He raised an eyebrow. "You sure?"

She nodded. "My job will be much easier having Wes and Dash onboard with the matchmaking. You and Robyn spoiled me. And I'll be bringing my tiara with me on future business trips."

Blaise grinned. "I will need proof of the tiara."

Hadley feigned shock. "You don't believe me."

He winked. "Send me a selfie the next time you're in New York."

"Deal." Because she now had his permission to text him a picture. "I hope your dinner goes well."

"It'll be boring." He sounded resigned. "But I'll be able to see a few clients I haven't seen in a while. Henry and Brett will be there, too."

"Great." Except it wasn't.

Saying goodbye didn't feel right, so she pressed her lips together.

Blaise rocked back on his heels. "Lex and Rizzo are waiting."

This was it. Hadley headed to the front door. Each step took effort. Her nerve endings twitched. Her heart pounded. She reached for the doorknob.

He did, too, his hand covering hers. "Take care of yourself."

She relished the feel of his warmth and the touch of his skin. "You, too."

He didn't move his hand. Neither did she. Hadley stood, feeling as if she were in limbo and not caring. Standing here for even the briefest amount of time was better than not seeing Blaise again.

"I should go," he said.

She nodded, but once again nothing happened. Her hand didn't want to turn the knob. His remained on top of hers.

"I—" she said.

"I—" he said at the same time.

"You go first," she offered.

His pulse was visible at his neck. "I don't want to say goodbye."

The tension between them disappeared. She blew out a breath. "I don't, either."

His mouth opened and then closed. "You don't date clients."

No, but he was more than a client. At least, she wanted him to be. And if she didn't take this chance, she might regret it. Forever. "I don't kiss clients, either, but I think it's time I made an exception to my rules."

Hadley rose on her toes and kissed Blaise, hard on the lips. She no longer cared about her rules or process. Only she and Blaise mattered.

He tensed for a nanosecond before relaxing into her kiss. As his mouth moved over hers, she soaked up his warmth and his taste. She'd forgotten how good he kissed, but she wanted to remember every detail.

His arms wrapped around Hadley, pulling her closer.

She went willingly, never letting her lips leave his.

As Blaise had all week, he made her feel special and adored. Cherished. She might be home, but she'd found a second home with him.

Slowly, he drew away from the kiss. "We should have been doing that all week."

"Germs."

He laughed before kissing her forehead. "Trust me, sweetheart, I wouldn't have cared."

Heat rose up her neck.

"When can I see you again?" he asked.

Hadley wiggled her toes. "I don't know, but I hope soon."

"Me, too." Blaise brushed his lips over hers. "We'll make this work."

She nodded, not knowing how when they lived in two different cities in two different states, but they had to try. She gazed into his eyes, seeing not only the possibilities but her future. "We will."

Chapter Fifteen

Blaise texted Hadley. Sometimes they spoke on the phone, but they always had a video chat in the evenings. He enjoyed hearing her voice and seeing her on the screen, but by week two of being apart, he was losing patience. He wanted to be with her. That gave him an idea.

Blaise: *I have a conference starting on Thursday in Las Vegas. Meet me there. I can send a plane.*
HL: *I could squeeze in a quick trip on Friday, but I'll save the planet and fly commercial.*
Blaise: *Send me your itinerary. I can't wait to see you.*
HL: *Same. I miss you.*

Let the countdown begin! He couldn't stop smiling.

Everyone from Trevor to his executive staff commented on Blaise's good mood. Most assumed the buzz surrounding the new fund was the reason, but it was Hadley.

His phone played *The Legend of Zelda* theme song. The ringtone belonged to Dash.

"Hey," Blaise answered. "What's going on?"

"I went on a date with a woman Hadley found for me. Dude, Raina is amazing." Awe filled Dash's voice. "She not only loves video games as much as I do, but she also designs them. We had a great time. We're getting together again before I leave for Las Vegas."

One down... Blaise grinned. "I'm so happy for you."

And he was, regardless of the bet, but knowing he was one step closer to winning thrilled him. And it was because of Hadley.

"It's only been one date, but so far Raina seems perfect," Dash said. "Hadley knows what she's doing."

Pride flowed through Blaise. "Yes, she does."

"Well, I just wanted to let you know and to say thanks."

"You're welcome." He crumpled a napkin into a ball and shot it into the garbage can. Score! Man, he loved winning. "Keep me posted."

"I will." Silence filled the line. "When do you see Hadley again?"

"Friday. She's meeting me in Las Vegas."

"Then I'll get to thank her in person," Dash said. "Talk to you later."

Blaise disconnected from the call. He leaned back in his chair and laughed. Everything was working out.

And soon he would have everything he wanted, including Hadley.

* * *

"You're in love with him."

Ignoring Fallon who sat on the bed, Hadley packed her clothes into her suitcase, crossing each item off her list as she went. The kids and Tiny were sound asleep. She had an afternoon flight tomorrow and couldn't wait to see Blaise. But…

In love with him?

Her heart wanted to answer one way. Her brain another..

She went with common sense. "We've haven't known each other long."

"You love him," Fallon repeated. "There's no timeframe for falling in love."

"Maybe there should be," Hadley mumbled because she'd never felt like this about any guy, even ones she'd dated for months.

"What did you say?" Fallon asked.

"I like Blaise. A lot." Hadley refolded a pair of pants. "I am falling for him."

"Fallen. Past tense." Fallon picked up the tiara

from the bed.

Hadley snatched it from her and packed the tiara between her pajamas. "And if I have?"

Compassion filled Fallon's eyes. "Be careful. I don't know what kind of contract you have with Blaise, but you've never dated a client before. It could make things murky."

Hadley had told Fallon enough to answer her sister's questions. The kids had told their mom that Mr. M was hiring Hadley to find him a wife.

"So far everything's been fine. We talk all the time." Blaise hadn't asked about her search for Wes and Dash, either. "I'm sure it'll be okay."

"But you're not one for breaking the rules."

Fallon knew her too well. Hadley plopped onto the bed.

"I'm not freaking out, if that's what you're worried about." Or hadn't been—but they also hadn't seen each other in person since he dropped her off at the condo. "But I'll be honest. If there wasn't so much money at stake, I'd be tempted to cancel our contract so he wasn't a client."

"Why don't you?" Lines creased Fallon's forehead. "It's just money, and you're never hurting for clients."

Hadley hadn't told her sister about the deal with Blaise. "The amount he's paying me is enough for us to buy a house nearby."

Fallon's eyes widened, both with surprise and

excitement. "Really?"

Hadley nodded. "It's a dream come true."

"But at what price?"

She shook her head. "It's not like I work at his company. Everything will be fine."

"If you're sure, but please be careful."

She thought about Blaise, his sweet smile and the heat in his eyes after he'd kissed her. "I am. And I will."

* * *

On Friday, as Hadley waited for her flight to board for Las Vegas, her phone rang. Wes Lockhart's name on the screen made her smile. He'd had a date last night with a woman Hadley thought would be perfect for him, and she couldn't wait to hear how it went. "Hi, Wes."

"Ready to join us in Las Vegas?"

All of Blaise's friends would be at the conference, but he'd promised they would spend time alone. She wouldn't be greedy as long as she got a kiss. Okay, a few kisses. Not to mention hugs. "I'm at the gate now."

"I wanted to talk to you without Blaise around." Wes sounded…troubled.

"What's going on?" She kept her voice light.

"I went on my date. Julia is a lovely woman. I can see why you chose her for me. Any other time…"

Hadley had heard this from clients before, but Wes had a reason why he felt this way. Or at least she thought he did. "It's not her, it's you?"

"I should be ready to date again, but I'm not." Wes sighed. "Or maybe I don't want to or… I don't know."

The mix of confusion and anguish in his voice made her want to reach through her phone and hug him. If only that were possible. "There are no shoulds. No one can decide when you're ready, only you."

"But the guys—"

"Care about you. They want what's best for you."

"Like we do with Blaise."

"Exactly. You've been through a lot with the cancer. You're young."

"Dash would beg to differ."

She laughed. "Okay, you're young compared to everyone but Dash."

That brought a laugh from Wes. "I just think I need more time to deal with everything I've been through."

"Then take it. There's no reason to rush."

"Blaise…"

"Do you want me to talk to him about it?"

"Would you?" Relief filled Wes's voice. "I was a jerk when he told us about his past, more out of being hurt he didn't trust me when I trusted him with everything when I was sick."

"He understands."

She had no doubt about that, but Blaise would have to realize Wes's well-being was more important than the bet. Because this was two separate issues. They just affected each other.

"How about I bring it up to him first?" she offered. "Pave the way so to speak?"

"That would be great. Thanks, Hadley."

A boarding announcement that included her row was made.

"I need to get on the plane."

"Have a good flight," Wes said. "I'm happy Blaise found you, Hadley. You're perfect for him."

"Thanks." Knowing his friend felt that way made her giddy, but she had no time to relish the feeling. She grabbed the handle of her suitcase. "I'll see you in Vegas."

* * *

The Golden Leaves Leadership Conference in Las Vegas brought out corporate people, entrepreneurs, investors, experts from a wide range of industries, and a few wannabes. From informative talks to extravagant dinners to deals made at the blackjack tables, the gathering was the stuff Blaise had dreamed about when he founded his company. Now, he would be one of the featured panelists later.

As if on cue, his friends walked up.

"Good luck on your panel, Blaise," Mason said.

Kieran grinned. "Knock 'em dead."

"Just remember who's done two panels," Wes joked.

"Dash?" Adam teased.

"Ha ha." Wes, however, wasn't smiling. "Wonderkid is off being interviewed. He doesn't do his second panel until tomorrow morning."

Adam rolled his eyes. "My bad."

Blaise listened to them, shifted his weight between his feet, fighting rising nerves.

Ridiculous.

He shouldn't be nervous. People loved hearing what Blaise Mortenson had to say. Except, unlike his five friends, he'd never spoken here before. This was his first invitation to participate on a panel. His friends might be kidding him now, but the board had told him how important this panel was.

An enormous deal.

Blaise didn't want to disappoint anyone.

"We're getting coffee," Mason said. "Want to join us?"

"No, thanks. I promised Brett I'd sit in on his session."

"That should get you psyched up for yours," Adam said.

"Or out," Wes joked.

Kieran shook his head. "Always the comedian, Lockhart."

As his friends headed toward the escalator, Blaise ran over what he wanted to say during his panel. He had bullet points on his tablet, but he'd memorized them.

"We need to talk." Lex pulled Blaise toward a less-crowded section of the lobby.

This wasn't like the guy. "What's wrong?"

A vein ticked at Lex's jaw. "That reporter is here."

That reporter meant the jerk who goaded Blaise into a fight. His fists clenched, so he flexed his fingers. Losing his temper would only upset the board again. And he had to remain in control for the panel.

Talk about lousy timing. "Keep him away from me."

"Will do, but you need to be aware that he's here and likely watching you."

Just what Blaise didn't need. He blew out a breath.

"I'll be careful." He'd learned his lesson about being provoked in public. The reporter probably wanted another fifteen minutes of fame after their last run-in. "Besides, that's why you and Rizzo are here."

Lex nodded once. "We've got your back."

A few hours later, Blaise hadn't seen the reporter. No one appeared to be lurking in the shadows or hallways. Maybe the guy was off bothering someone else and would leave Blaise alone. Lex was in the auditorium where the panel would be held. Rizzo was nearby, waiting in a long line for the coffee Blaise wanted.

His cell phone buzzed.

HL: *I'm here. Picked up my badge.*
Blaise: *I'm on the second level of the South Hall, hanging out before my panel.*
HL: *On my way.*

She was here. On her way to him. Blaise put his phone in his jacket pocket.

Anticipation buzzed through him. He couldn't wait to see her.

If anyone could calm him before his panel, she could.

Being apart hadn't been easy, but the distance between San Francisco and Portland wasn't a deal-breaker. It beat the alternative—not being together.

Blaise searched the people coming onto the second floor but didn't see her. He rubbed his palms together.

She would be here soon.

Not soon enough.

He nearly laughed aloud.

Blaise hadn't been looking for a girlfriend or a relationship, but he'd found both in Hadley. He couldn't imagine his life without his beautiful, smart, demanding matchmaker.

They were perfect together.

He fixed problems. She made plans. Together, they would find a solution that worked for everyone, including her family. Until then, they would make the most of whatever time they had, especially here in Las Vegas once he finished his panel.

He picked a speck of lint off his jacket.

"Blaise!" Hadley called out from the escalator.

He waved at her, and she hurried toward him.

Hadley's auburn hair shone underneath the lights. She wore jeans, a nice blouse, and boots. A lanyard with a badge hung around her neck.

She smiled at him, and his pulse stuttered.

Blaise wove his way around people to meet her halfway. "Hey."

"Hey, you." Her blue eyes twinkled. "Having fun?"

"Now I am." He brushed his lips across hers before hugging her. She smelled like sunshine and strawberries. "I've missed you."

"Same." He ran his hand over her soft hair, needing to touch her. "We're together now."

"As soon as my panel is over, I'm all yours. There's a party later, but we can skip it."

"I don't care what we do as long as we're together."

That sounded good to him. All he wanted was to stand here and stare. Seeing her settled him the way he knew it would. She was so beautiful, but she'd also worked this morning before flying to him this afternoon. "Are you hungry? Do you want a drink?"

Hadley touched his arm, connecting them in a way he hadn't known he needed. "You're all I need."

"I need another kiss." Blaise's lips touched hers, harder this time. His mouth lingered, tasting her sweetness and her warmth. Yes, she was exactly what he needed.

He knew people were around them, the din of conversations, but he didn't care. He had nothing to hide.

Not anymore. Not with Hadley.

Blaise didn't want to wait to kiss her. He needed her.

As he pulled her closer, she arched against him. He didn't want to stop kissing her, but there would be time for more kisses later. This was only the beginning for them.

No rush.

That was what he'd been telling himself.

And he repeated the words, even if quiet desperation for her flowed through him.

Slowly, he drew the kiss to an end, but he didn't back away.

Blaise couldn't. Instead, he rested his forehead against hers. "I could get used to doing this all the time."

"Me, too." She sounded breathless.

Good. That was how he felt around her. He laced his fingers with hers, wanting to hold on to her tightly.

Not that he planned on letting her go.

An announcement about the upcoming session sounded.

He tugged on his tie with his free hand.

"Are you okay?" she asked.

"Yes, I just want the panel to go well."

She kissed his cheek. "You'll be brilliant as usual."

Her compliment was what he needed.

"So…" they said at the same time and then laughed.

"You go first," she said.

"Dash likes the woman you introduced him to," Blaise said. "He went out with her again."

Hadley's face brightened. "I'm happy to hear that. They are an excellent match, so I'm curious how it plays out."

"He will put a ring on her finger and say 'I do.'"

She laughed. "I appreciate your confidence in my abilities, but don't tell Dash that or he might freak out."

"He'll get there."

"Don't you guys call him Mr. Status Quo?"

"Yes, but he's never dated a woman who designs video games or gone out with the same person twice in one week," Blaise explained. "You hit a home run."

She beamed. "I can't wait to see what happens in the next inning."

The doors to where his panel was being held

opened. People streamed out from the previous session and into the lobby where they stood. Blaise noticed Rizzo still in line for coffee, but now the crowd was between them.

"I saw Wes earlier, but he didn't mention his date." Blaise wanted to get his mind off the panel. "Did he tell you anything?"

As her smile faltered, she glanced around. "This might not be the best place to talk."

He didn't see anyone paying attention to them. "It's fine."

She took a breath. "Wes went out on his date, but he doesn't want to go on another with her."

"Did something happen?"

"No, he liked her. It's just not the right time for him to be dating."

That didn't sound like Wes. "Yeah, right."

"He was honest with me," Hadley said, her tone compassionate. "The last couple of years have been hard on him. Physically and emotionally. He wants more time before he jumps into the dating world again. It's good he recognizes that because I think he needs a break."

"What he needs is to move on with his life," Blaise countered. "The cancer is in remission. He needs a wife."

Her jaw clenched. "He's not ready for a date. A wife is the last thing he needs."

No. Hadley was being stubborn. Maybe she was

following a flowchart or something, but Blaise wouldn't let anything get in his way of winning. "Wes has always been up for going out and dating."

"Maybe before, but that's not what he wants now. It's not right to push him into something because you want it to happen."

"He told you all this?"

She nodded. "We spoke on the phone."

That was strange. Blaise didn't like how easy she spoke about Wes. "He didn't say a word to me."

"He will." Hadley sounded certain. "It's too bad, but trying to find someone to date right now would be a waste of my time and your money."

Heat rushed up Blaise's neck. "The bet—"

"What's more important to you? Winning the bet or doing what's best for your friend?"

He didn't like the accusation in her voice or how close—familiar—she suddenly appeared to be with Wes. "They aren't mutually exclusive. Which is why I hired you."

"Talk to Wes. Hear what he has to say."

"Wes is my friend, not yours. So I'm not sure why he's discussing this with you."

She gave Blaise a funny look. "I'm his matchmaker."

"Then you should know love is what he needs. Find him another date as soon as you're back in the office."

Something flashed in her eyes. "I can't."

I can't.

Memories slammed into Blaise like a speeding semi-truck with no brakes, roaring in his ears and making him nauseous. His parents had said the same thing to him when they chose heroin over him. Time and time again. All he'd ever wanted was to be important enough for someone to put him first, to choose him. He thought Hadley felt that way about him. But she was choosing Wes.

Not me.

"You can't?" Blaise repeated, not believing what was happening.

"I can't because that's not what Wes needs. Give him time to heal emotionally first."

What Wes needed? Blaise grimaced. What about him?

Each muscle tensed into a rock-hard ball. Anger flared, his temper spiraling out of control.

He'd been wrong about Hadley. She didn't care about him.

Not at all.

If she did, she would have picked him. Not Wes.

"I hired you to do a job." Blaise spoke through gritted teeth. "Now you're telling me you won't do it?"

She flinched. "I'm trying to do the right thing."

"For Wes. What about for me?"

"For both of you."

Not good enough. Not even close. "The right

thing is for you to what I hired you to do."

"I can't."

Blaise hated those two words. Why had he thought Hadley was different? She wasn't.

He raised his chin. "Then I'll hire someone else."

Her jaw dropped. "You're firing me?"

"I am." The words sounded harsh to his ears, but they would never work out. He saw that now. "I hired you for your matchmaking skills. Now, you're telling me you can't do the job. Yes, I'm firing you because Matched by Lowell is nothing but a scam. I'll find a more qualified matchmaker who won't give up when things don't work out the first time."

"He's not ready." She choked out the words, her voice was whisper soft.

"Yes, he is."

Her eyebrows drew together, matching the pinched expression on her face. "Winning is that important to you?"

"If you knew me the way I thought you did, you would know what the bet means to me."

Hurt filled her eyes. "If you knew me the way I thought you did, you would know why I can't do this to Wes."

Blaise didn't—couldn't—say anything.

She swallowed. "So where does that leave us?"

"There is no us." The words shot out. "If there was, we'd never be having this discussion. We got carried away pretending to be together. That's all."

Hadley's eyes gleamed. She took a breath and then another. "That's all."

She sounded so defeated.

Blaise didn't—couldn't—care. He pressed his lips together. He had nothing to say to her.

"I offer a money back guarantee. I'll void our contract and refund the retainer you paid me." With that, she hurried away from him, disappearing into the crowd.

He stood, paralyzed. People rode the escalators. Some entered the room where he'd be speaking on the panel. Others talked as he and Hadley had.

Except they hadn't been chatting or catching up.

They'd fought.

Broken up.

And...

Blaise rubbed the spot over his heart.

I can't.

Her words had slayed him. Hurt him deeper than he'd thought possible.

Until meeting Hadley, he hadn't known how much he needed someone in his life—in his heart—but she'd chosen someone else. Now he was on his own again.

Alone.

And he didn't know what to do.

Chapter Sixteen

"Men suck." Fallon's angry voice was so loud Hadley had to pull her phone away from her ear. "Blaise is no different from the rest of them."

Tears stung Hadley's eyes. She'd hoped—believed—Blaise would be different. If she hadn't, she would have never fallen in...

An announcement sounded—the boarding call for a Boston flight.

She blinked. Wiped her eyes. Tried to pull herself together.

Falling apart in the hotel room she'd checked into only hours ago had been hard enough. She couldn't lose it here—in public at the airport.

And wait...

What Fallon said didn't sound right.

Hadley sniffled before readjusting the phone at her ear. "I thought you weren't going to blame all men for the actions of one. Or two."

"Maybe tomorrow I'll feel differently," Fallon explained, her tone harsh. "But right now? I hate them all."

A family of four ran toward the end of the terminal. The kids wore brightly colored backpacks. The man pulled a suitcase behind him. The mom held on to the hand of a young boy. A little girl carried a stuffed llama that was identical to Audra's.

Hadley's chest tightened. She swallowed past the burning in her throat. "I wish I were home."

"You will be soon."

The line of people standing at the counter told Hadley she wasn't the only one trying to get to San Francisco tonight. "If not this flight, then the next one."

"You'll get on."

"I will." Hadley needed to think positively. The thought of being stuck in the same city as Blaise filled her eyes with tears. She blinked them away.

A part of her wished she'd stayed in her hotel room with a box of tissues, a pint of cookie dough ice cream, and her tiara on her head, but she could do the same thing with Fallon once Hadley arrived home.

Ice cream might not solve problems, but it wouldn't make them worse. The disappointment, anger, and disdain in Blaise's eyes had cut her to the core. And what he'd said…

Trying to calm herself, she inhaled, held her breath, and then exhaled.

"You're too quiet," Fallon said. "Talk to me. Tell me what you're thinking."

The only thing that matters to Blaise is winning.

He'd said that to Hadley, more than once.

But she'd forgotten.

And she couldn't tell Fallon. Blaise was still her client. Even if he wasn't, she would never betray his confidence or privacy. Wes's, either.

"As long as I did what he wanted, things were fine. When I wouldn't…"

"That tells me the man isn't as smart as everyone thinks," Fallon said in a matter-of-fact tone. "You, my dear sister, are a catch. Not only that, you care about others. Your family, friends, clients. If Blaise can't see that, then the man is an idiot and doesn't deserve you."

"Thanks." Hadley had been positive he would understand about Wes. She was disappointed Blaise hadn't, but she'd never expected things to explode the way they did. "I feel so stupid."

"I only met him the one time, but he fooled the kids."

Her heart dropped. Audra and Ryder had enjoyed spending time with Blaise.

"Before you worry about Audra and Ryder, they only saw him twice. They know he lives in another state. It's no big deal."

Except this was another guy disappearing from their lives. Hadley wouldn't introduce any men to them again. Not until she knew…

Knew what? That a relationship would last? That the feelings were real? That her love wasn't unrequited?

Love.

A sob escaped.

"Hey." Fallon's voice softened. "It'll get better. Even though it feels like you're sinking and will never be okay again, you will be. You want to know how I know that?"

"How?"

"Because my smart sister told me that when I didn't want to get out of bed ever again," Fallon said. "And you were right. Every day gets better. And one day, we're both going to meet men who are different from those in our past. They won't be perfect, but they will be what each of us needs. And the heartache and pain we've suffered will make the upcoming happy times worth it."

Hadley hoped so. Though "one day" would be a long time for her. Her heart needed to recover. "Thanks."

"And you know what?"

"What?" she asked.

"Someday, Blaise will regret what he lost."

Wait. Fallon didn't know about the bet. Even if

she knew about it, the bet was still going on. "He hasn't lost anything."

"I meant you, silly."

Hadley inhaled sharply.

"I hate how this turned out for you," Fallon said. "But each heartbreak brings you one step closer to finding true love."

An elderly couple strolled by with their hands linked. Love radiated between them.

That's what I wanted.

What I thought I found with Blaise.

Except Hadley had been fooling herself to think they belonged together. The billionaire and the matchmaker. Both with companies to run in different states and a family who needed her. "I was daydreaming. Getting caught up in the fairy tale."

"I don't blame you," Fallon admitted. "It was a good fairy tale while it lasted. But there's a happy ending out there for you and for me."

Fallon deserved one. And…

So do I.

"Someday…" Hadley said.

"Someday," her sister repeated.

A happily ever after required work, commitment, and love.

When the time was right and her heart was ready, Hadley would find a man who wanted the same as her.

Another announcement sounded.

"They're boarding my flight," Hadley said. "I need to listen to the names called off the standby list. I'll let you know."

"I'm here if you need me."

Her sister was the best. "Thanks."

"Your heart *will* stop hurting so bad."

Hadley sighed. She only wished it would stop hurting now.

* * *

Somehow, Blaise survived the panel. He barely remembered a word he'd said or a question he'd answered, but he'd received nothing but praise about the session. Someone had taped it, and he could confirm whether or not he'd made a lovesick fool out of himself.

Not lovesick.

A fool with a capital F.

Which was why he now sat alone in the VIP area of the hottest new club in Las Vegas. He didn't drink much, but tonight he would get blackout drunk. Maybe then he could stop hurting.

He admired the bottle sitting on the table: 23 Year Old Pappy Van Winkle Family Reserve Kentucky Straight Bourbon Whiskey. An empty glass was within arm's reach. His bodyguards hovered with concerned expressions on their faces, but Lex and Rizzo knew to leave Blaise alone.

He poured two fingers of the amber red liquid and downed the contents. The bourbon burned, but that didn't keep him from refilling the glass and doing the same thing until he lost track of how many drinks he'd had. He filled the glass once again, only this time to the top and drank as much as he could in one gulp.

"Drinking alone?" Wes stood next to the table, towering over Blaise. "Or strategizing with yourself on who I could marry so you can win the bet?"

The words hit Blaise like a sucker punch. A million and one thoughts collided in his brain. Most of them bad. A nice buzz was on the way, and he didn't want it to stop. He refilled his glass before placing the bottle on the table.

Playing dumb wasn't his usual MO, but in this case, he had nothing else to try. "I have no idea what you're talking about."

Wes half laughed, though no humor flashed in his eyes. "The video of you firing Hadley has gone viral."

"What video?"

Wes pulled out his phone, touched the screen, and shoved his cell phone at Blaise. "I had no idea you wanted to win this badly."

Words sat on the tip of Blaise's tongue, ready to jump out in his defense. But he pressed his lips together, took the phone from Wes, and hit *play*.

Whoever held the camera stood behind a potted plant. The sound quality was poor, but the filming showed him kissing Hadley. Blaise hadn't noticed anyone with a camera, but he hadn't been paying attention to the people around them.

As he watched, a knot in his stomach grew. Not all their words could be heard, but enough to imply what was happening.

Blaise swore under his breath. He'd gotten sloppy. Let down his guard. All because of his wanting to be with Hadley.

She was radiant. Her smile lit up her face with pure happiness and joy. Only that disappeared the longer they spoke. When he fired her—everything he'd said then was clear in the video—Hadley paled as if she might collapse. Her expression turned to a portrait of pain and sadness.

He drank more.

"So it's true." Hard lines formed around Wes's mouth. "You hired Hadley to find Dash and me wives. You pretended to date her so she could get to know us. You set us up."

Even though Wes wasn't asking questions, Blaise nodded once to acknowledge the truth.

Except one thing had been true—his feelings for her were real. He might have told her they were pretending, but if they had been, he wouldn't be feeling so miserable and wanting to numb the pain.

Wes's nostrils flared. "You always said winning was everything, so I understand your motivation. We all compete, even if it's unspoken. But after the time we spent together during my treatments, you were the one who was there the most with me, I thought we were friends, best friends."

"We are." The words erupted from Blaise's mouth.

"Then how does a matchmaker you hired know me better than you do?"

"I…"

"Hadley's correct. I'm not ready to date. She tried to tell you, but you wouldn't listen. You didn't care." Wes snatched the phone from Blaise. "Not about me. Or Dash. The only thing that matters to you is winning the bet."

Guilt coated Blaise's mouth. Not even the expensive bourbon could wash it away. "I'm sorry."

"Are you?" Wes's voice was harsh.

"Yes. I only wanted…" *To win.* "What I want doesn't matter any longer."

"You haven't lost the bet."

No, but Blaise had lost something else.

He reached for the bottle and refilled the glass.

Wes shook his head. "So that's how tonight will be? Drink until you puke?"

The less Blaise remembered of today, the better. This time, however, he only sipped from his glass. The liquor had warmed his blood. His buzz was getting stronger. He just needed…more.

Wes sighed. "While your brain is still halfway functioning, tell me who you have on Hadley."

Blaise blinked. "Huh?"

"Security."

He glanced at Lex and Rizzo. "No one."

Wes swore under his breath. "Where is she?"

"Don't know." Blaise took another sip. "Don't care."

He didn't want to care. A few more drinks and he wouldn't.

"Stop being an idiot." Wes grabbed the glass away from him, splashing bourbon on the table. "You're not the only one on the video that's gone viral. You mention her company's name. You can see her face. A simple search will tell everyone who she is. If the media wants to find her…"

The press might accost her, try to get a sound bite or an interview. Blaise had just seen their kiss. He could almost feel her lips against his. And…

His heart plummeted to his feet.

Anyone seeing Hadley's face would know she cared about him. Someone out there—someone not so nice like the person who filmed them—could hurt her to get to him.

"I have to find her." He stood, swayed, fell back against the booth.

"You're in no shape to go after her." Wes had every right to laugh at Blaise, but he didn't. Instead, he motioned to Lex and Rizzo. "Find Hadley and bring her to Blaise. We need to make sure she's safe."

"Blaise?" Lex asked.

The club moved like a boat. Maybe he'd drunk

too much too fast. Blaise closed his eyes, willing everything to freeze for a minute, including the alcohol wreaking havoc in his bloodstream. "What Wes said."

"We'll get you to your hotel first," Rizzo said.

"I'm…" Blaise wasn't fine. He was hurting, and all his money couldn't fix what was wrong. "Go. Now."

Wes stepped forward. "You heard him. I'll get Blaise back to his hotel suite, and I'll make sure he stays there until one of you returns."

Wes was a good friend.

Blaise wasn't. "I'm sorry."

"I know." Wes helped him stand. "Let's get you out of here."

Blaise reached for the bottle.

Wes pulled him away from the table. "Nuh-huh. The only thing you need is water and Hadley."

"She chose you over me."

"No, you big old lump. Hadley wasn't choosing me."

Wes walked him toward the exit, each step took effort and more than once Blaise thought he would stumble, but Wes kept him upright.

"She was doing the right thing, trying to help you realize what's important," Wes continued. "It's not the bet, in case you missed that."

Blaise groaned. "I screwed up."

"Big-time."

"I need to know she's safe."

"Once we're at the hotel, I'll get my security on it, too, but Lex and Rizzo will find her."

If she was still in town. Blaise couldn't see Hadley throwing herself a pity party. He doubted she was in Las Vegas because he'd given her no reason to stay.

He swayed, his world kept tilting. But all he could see was the video, playing in a continuous loop in his drunken mind.

He'd fired her. Told her everything between them was pretend. Kicked her out of his life.

All he'd wanted was to win, but he'd lost.

Lost so much.

Lost…everything.

* * *

Could this day get any worse?

Not even ten o'clock on a Saturday, and five clients had told Hadley her matchmaking services were no longer required. All requested refunds because she had a money-back guarantee. In seven years, no one had asked for their money back.

Until today.

She squeezed her eyes shut to keep from crying.

Audra and Ryder sat on the couch, watching a cartoon. Their cereal bowls were on the coffee table next to half-full cups of orange juice. The smiles on their young faces told Hadley they were oblivious to how awful she felt.

Good. She wanted to keep it that way.

Ten more emails sat in her inbox. Four voice messages had been left on her cell phone. And she was afraid to open or listen to any of them. The courage she used to start the business had deserted her.

She hated that.

Hated that she didn't know how to bravely face what was happening. But no matter how much the optimist in her wanted to believe those clients who'd emailed or called wanted to support her, she couldn't.

Because of Blaise and that video clip.

Then I'll hire someone else.

You're firing me?

I am. I hired you for your matchmaking skills. Now, you're telling me you can't do the job. Yes, I'm firing you because Matched by Lowell is nothing but a scam. I'll find a more qualified matchmaker who won't give up when things don't work out the first time.

Her life's work destroyed in seconds by a badly filmed video shot. She only wished she could laugh.

Maybe someday.

But not today.

Blaise Mortenson had stomped on her heart and decimated her business with the precision of a neurosurgeon with a robotic scalpel. Even if Hadley wanted to defend herself, she couldn't because she needed to protect her clients' privacy even if in doing so she hurt herself and her livelihood.

The same word of mouth that had made her business a success was now destroying it, tearing down her years of hard work. By the end of the day, she might not have any clients left. That would mean the end of the Matched by Lowell.

Hadley glanced out the condo's living room window to the street below. Matched by Lowell was sinking faster than the Titanic, yet she had a black SUV parked in front of her building with at least one, possibly two, bodyguards inside.

"Should you take the guys cups of coffee?" Fallon asked.

"I don't know bodyguard protocol. Who knows if the same guys from last night are here this morning? I want to tell whoever it is to leave," she said. "That we don't need protection."

"You don't know if that's true or not," Fallon countered. "After what happened at the airport…"

Two reporters had been waiting for her when she got off the plane in San Francisco, but so had Jackson, who introduced himself as the head of Blaise's security team and explained concerns over her safety following a video going viral. He'd whisked her out of the airport and into a waiting SUV driven by Kai, another man she'd never seen before. Yet, she was grateful for them getting her home safely.

"I know, but I can't afford—"

"Blaise is paying. Isn't that what Jackson said?"

Which was the problem. The thought of Blaise spending a penny on Hadley made her stomach churn. "I don't want to feel obligated to Blaise."

"Then don't. He's the one who put you in this situation. I watched the video." Fallon sounded almost guilty. "The guy acted like a jerk. He slammed your business. He owes you."

The kids giggled at something on the TV.

Hadley didn't want to bring up her work—or what could soon be the lack of it—in front of them.

"He doesn't owe me anything. I should have pressed harder for us to talk privately. I didn't, so the video is on me, too."

"Nothing should be on you, sis."

Except it was. Hadley stared at Audra and Ryder, who laughed at their show. If anything happened to the kids…

Hadley forced herself to breathe. "This doesn't involve only me. Until we know more of what's going on and if there will be any issues, having someone watch the condo is smart. Once it's over, nothing will be left tying me to Blaise."

Not that there had been anything between them.

We got carried away pretending to be together. That's all.

At least not on his side.

Her eyes burned.

She stared up at the ceiling and blinked.

Hadley's cell phone buzzed. She glanced at the screen.

Blaise: *You ok?*

Hadley laughed. It was do that or cry. Her heart ached. Her eyes hurt. And she needed a bodyguard outside the condo building.

None of this was okay.

She took a breath and another before turning over her phone so the screen didn't show.

"It's him," Fallon said. "I can tell by your expression."

"Doesn't matter. I have nothing to say to him." Hadley had refunded his six-figure retainer when she woke up this morning. Not that two hours of sleep was much.

Her phone buzzed again.

She ignored it.

The buzzing continued.

Hadley sighed. "I'll read his text so it stops trying to notify me."

Blaise: *Can we please talk?*

That seemed like the worst idea in the world. She knew where she stood with him.

Nowhere.

Another buzz.

Blaise: *I'm sorry. Please, Hadley. Call me.*

Despite everything, a part of her wanted to talk to him, but she couldn't. Not after what he'd said.

There was only one thing to do.

She blocked his number.

Hadley stared at her niece and nephew, each covered with a fleece throw. Her sister had her laptop open and stared at the screen.

This—these three people and Tiny—were all Hadley needed. She might have dreamed of a happily ever after, but what she had with her sister and the kids would be enough.

It had to be.

* * *

The first time Blaise had woken up in his hotel room, Rizzo was sitting in a chair watching him. According to the bodyguard, Hadley was safe in San Francisco and being watched. The news brought relief but also regret because she was supposed to be with Blaise.

He must have fallen asleep again because he woke up again with Lex in his room instead. The bodyguard handed Blaise a glass of water and acetaminophen. Neither of which did much for his pounding head so he closed his eyes again.

The third time Blaise woke up, he felt as if someone was jackhammering his brain. He was also sober enough to know he'd made a huge mistake. Several, actually. But the biggest one he needed to fix.

Now.

So he'd sent texts.

He didn't blame Hadley for not replying, so he called. It went straight to voice mail.

Was she asleep?

Or ignoring him?

Probably the latter, but he would try again. He sent another text. Maybe she would reply to this one. Except…

It didn't go through like the others had.

His stomach roiled.

Blaise threw his phone. It bounced off the bed and landed on the carpeted floor.

"Did she block you?" Wes asked, who was now sitting in the same chair as Rizzo and Lex had earlier.

"Yes, she blocked me." The dark circles under Wes's eyes suggested he'd slept little, but his hair was damp. "Were you here all night?"

"No. Your security team babysat you after they returned to the hotel. They needed showers and food this morning, so I'm here."

"Lucky you." Blaise studied Wes, but the guy's stoic expression gave away nothing. "Does you being here mean we're still friends?"

"I don't hate you if that's what you're asking."

"You're disappointed."

"Very."

Hate might have been easier to deal with. "Have I apologized?"

"More times than you want to know. Dash turned off his phone after you drunk dialed him a hundred times."

"A hundred?"

"Twelve."

That wasn't much better.

"Everyone will be here soon," Wes said. "Henry and Brett, too."

Blaise stiffened. "Why?"

"Because they're worried. I am, too." Wes rested his elbows on his thighs and leaned forward. "You've never acted the way you did yesterday. With Hadley. Or at the club."

"It was a bad day."

"You've had those before and never been like this."

"One time, I bought a helicopter."

"And I've bought toys, too. But you've always guarded your privacy. The Blaise I know would have never kissed a woman out in the open like you did."

"I was nervous about the panel, and I missed her so much. I wasn't thinking."

"Which isn't like you."

That was true. He nodded.

"The Blaise I know wouldn't have fired her or anyone so publicly."

"She said something that reminded me of my parents." An excuse, yes, but the truth. He'd lost control and lashed out, not caring who got hurt. "I couldn't think or see straight."

"The Blaise I know would never have set out to get blackout drunk on purpose. I've never seen you drink like that. Given your parents..."

Wes's worried tone shattered Blaise. "That was the first time. I've never done anything like that before. I don't plan on doing it again. Again, I wasn't thinking straight. No harm done."

"To you."

"What do you mean?" Blaise asked.

"You single-handedly destroyed Matched by Lowell."

"How?"

"The video."

The video. Right. His chin dropped to his chest. "I only remember parts of it."

"You called out her company. Fired her. Rumor has it clients are leaving in droves and asking for refunds."

Blaise buried his face in his hands. Hadley had trusted him. She'd told him about her exes, but he'd done the same thing. No, he'd hurt her more, destroying the business she'd built. "I can't believe I did that. What was I thinking? I wasn't. That's the problem. I need to help her."

"Blaise."

He lowered his hands to look at Wes, who stared at him with an unreadable expression on his face. "Breathe."

Blaise did.

"Why do you need to help Hadley?" Wes asked.

"This is my fault. Helping her is the right thing to do."

"Giving her money is an easy fix."

"It is, but money can't repair her business's reputation." Blaise knew what could. "I need to go to San Francisco and make this right. I think…I love her."

Wes's eyebrows rose. He tilted his head. "What are you going to do?"

"I have no idea." Blaise brushed his hand through his hair. "I'm afraid to make another mistake. Yesterday, I let the past with my parents and my jealousy of you get in the way. I acted like a madman. Now, I've lost the woman I love and ruined her business. I don't deserve her. I'm sure I've blown my chance with her, but I have to help her. She might not want me back, but I can't leave her with nothing."

The edges of Wes's mouth curved slightly. "You don't have to do this on your own. I'm in. The others will be, too."

Blaise swallowed. He wasn't used to accepting help. He never wanted help. Hiring Hadley had been a necessity to win the bet, but now…

He doubted he could pull this off without the others. "Good, because I need help."

Wes smile spread. "That's what friends are for."

Blaise had the best friends in the world. They

were his family, and he loved each one of them—Adam, Dash, Kieran, Mason, Wes, Henry, and Brett. They weren't the calvary though they each could buy one if needed. Blaise smiled. "It might take all of us to figure a way to get me out of this mess."

"But we will. Because that's what we do for each other. Especially when one of us is in trouble." Wes winked. "Of his own making."

Blaise laughed. He had no idea what would happen next, but he wasn't in this alone. His friends would do what they could to help him with Hadley. And those same friends would be there for him.

Whether he succeeded or failed.

But Blaise hoped he succeeded because, despite how he'd hurt Hadley, he had a feeling she needed him as much as he needed her.

Chapter Seventeen

Shoulders hunched, Hadley entered her office. No sense of pride or accomplishment flowed through her this Monday morning. Only regret. She'd put her dream of buying a house ahead of her company. She'd broken her rules and trusted her heart. She only had one person to blame for what had happened—herself.

Blaise's harsh words about her company would fade from people's memories. She just didn't know how long that would take—a week, a month, six months?

Would more clients leave?

Would Matched by Lowell survive?

If not, how long could she live off her savings?

That, Hadley realized, was her biggest fear—to find herself unable to support her family. She wouldn't put her sister and the kids into another situation where they lost their home. Which was why last night, after everyone had gone to bed, Hadley had searched for a second job where she could work while trying to salvage her company. She hadn't applied, but that was on her to-do list. She needed to update her resume first—something she hadn't done since she started her business.

Her eyes were gritty, but touching them would make it worse. She'd cried so much, not even cold compresses and cucumber slices could help the swelling and redness.

That didn't stop her from forcing a smile now. She didn't want Ella to worry. Hadley had been doing enough of that for the both of them.

She went to her assistant's desk. "Any calls or messages?"

The worry in Ella's dark gaze didn't bode well. "Yes."

Hadley's insides twisted. She didn't have to be a mind reader to know the news wouldn't be good. "More clients want out."

Ella nodded. "I'm pulling their contracts for you."

Hadley's stomach hardened, but she wouldn't lose hope. Not yet. "How many are left?"

"Three."

She didn't think her heart could break more. She was wrong. A tsunami of turmoil tore her up inside, but she needed to be strong. Ella counted on this job.

Hadley raised her chin, attempting to appear in control when her world was imploding around her. "Those three will have our undivided attention."

Finding clients through word of mouth might not be enough any longer. She'd never had to advertise, but she would if it meant her business survived.

The corners of Ella's mouth curved. "Until new clients sign up."

Follow Ella's lead.

Think positively.

"All three left messages of support, saying they are fully committed to you," Ella continued as if knowing Hadley needed to hear good news. "Jonathon is excited about his date tomorrow night and wants you to call him. Sounds like he might need a pep talk."

Jonathon was a sweet, bookish intellectual from New York. He'd made his money off patents. He hated living alone in what he jokingly called the ivory tower, a high-rise apartment building in the heart of Manhattan. He wanted to share his life with a woman who adored books and cats. "I'll call him."

"He wanted to know if you'll be in New York next week in case he needs more dating practice."

The smart move would be to say no, but Hadley still had a client on the East Coast, which meant she would travel there as planned. "I will."

"I'm glad to hear that." Ella sat taller. "Business as usual."

Hadley nodded, afraid of how her voice might sound if she spoke.

"Leila called to say Travis is the one." Ella beamed. "They're going out again this weekend."

"Wonderful." Leila was the CEO of a retail chain based in the Midwest. In her late thirties, she'd taken over the company for her father. Now that she'd expanded and doubled revenue, she didn't want her priority in life to be work. She wanted to find love. "I'll call her for an update."

"Geoff wants to know how he can help."

Of course he did. Warmth centered above Hadley's heart. Geoff lived two blocks away from her in the Marina District. He worked at an investment firm that was a rival of Clint's former one, but unlike her ex-brother-in-law, Geoff was the definition of a nice guy. He would be perfect for Fallon, if she was ready to date. But she wasn't, so Hadley would keep looking for his love match. "I'll call him, too."

"You'll find new clients."

"I intend to." Hadley was straddling the line between remaining positive and being in denial. "But put together a resume. I will see this through to the bitter end if need be, but I don't want you to find yourself jobless."

The day dragged.

She'd spoken to each of her three clients. Then, she'd canceled contracts and refunded retainers for the rest. She was honoring her money-back guarantee even if a few were taking advantage of the policy, given she'd introduced them to their future spouses and the wedding invitations were in the mail.

A lesson learned.

An expensive one.

The office phone kept ringing. The calls were from the media, wanting to ask her questions or requesting an interview.

By the time four o'clock rolled around, Hadley was wiped out. She slumped in her chair, trying to see past the tears brimming in her eyes. She hadn't cried yet today, and she didn't want to.

"Hadley?" Ella stood in the doorway. "Henry Davenport is in the lobby. He wants to see you."

Seriously? Hadley had no idea what the guy wanted unless he was canceling their arrangement, too. "Send him back and then go home. We've done all we can today."

"Tomorrow is a brand-new day. We will survive." Ella's optimism never faded. "You built the company from scratch. You'll do it again. I have faith in you."

"I appreciate the support and your confidence. I hope you know I'll give you a glowing recommendation if needed."

Ella shook her head. "You're not getting rid of me that easily. I appreciate the offer, and I will update my resume, but I don't think I'll need to use it."

Gratitude washed over Hadley. She was so lucky to have Ella. "See you tomorrow."

Her assistant grinned. "You can count on it, boss."

Hearing "boss" reminded Hadley of Lex and Rizzo.

And…Blaise.

Something pressed hard against her chest. She forced herself to breathe, but it wasn't easy. Even after everything that had happened with Blaise, her heart missed him. She missed him.

And that made her feel like an idiot.

She wanted—no, needed—to forget about him. It would take time, but she hoped not too much.

The office phone rang. Hadley grimaced. The media sure was persistent, but she'd told Ella at three o'clock to let all calls go to voice mail. They could delete the messages tomorrow morning.

A few minutes later, Henry strolled in wearing a designer suit and looking as if he'd just stepped off the pages of a glossy fashion magazine.

Hadley stood. "I wasn't expecting you."

Henry walked around the desk and hugged her.

She wanted to cling to him but fought the urge and let go of him.

He stepped away from her. "Rough day?"

Nodding, she motioned to the chair on the opposite side of the desk. "What brings you to San Francisco?"

"I was compelled to come." Henry sat. His gaze was earnest. "I'm sorry for what happened with

Blaise."

She forced herself not to react and sat. "Thank you, but it's not your fault."

"I recommended you to him."

"Still not your fault." She kept her voice steady. At least she hoped that was how she sounded. "An apology isn't necessary."

"I've heard rumors about your business."

As if on cue, the office phone rang again. She would have lots of messages to delete.

"They're true." Hadley had nothing to hide. No doubt what she'd worked so hard to build was now a punch line over drinks. "I have a handful of clients left. Three to be exact. And yes, it's as bad as it sounds."

As his eyebrows drew together, he leaned forward. "What are you going to do?"

She shrugged. "Try to salvage this somehow. If I can't, close and find a new job."

Henry straightened. "Then my timing is perfect."

"For what?"

He beamed. "Bringing you a new client."

Affection for her friend overflowed. Henry might be eccentric, but his heart was made of gold. "That's sweet of you, but we both know you're not interested in a relationship. Hosting your own birthday party each year is the only commitment you want to make."

His laughter filled her office. "You know me well. I enjoy having an uncomplicated life. I do what I want and don't have to worry about anybody else. Which is why I'm not the one who wants your services."

"Then who?"

"He wants a nondisclosure agreement signed first." Henry removed sheets of paper folded in thirds. "He takes his privacy seriously, especially in matters of the heart."

"Not a problem."

The office line rang again. Man, these reporters needed to get a life and stop preying on people like her.

She read through the pages. A blank space had been left for the client's legal name. "I'm used to these forms, but you know I work a certain way."

"I explained you have a unique way of doing business and he must talk to you in person before you take him on. He's fine with that."

There was one thing she had to ask. "Did he see the video that went viral?"

"Yes. He has, shall we say, specific needs, and we believe you're the only one who can help him."

"Specific needs or requests appear to be my specialty."

Henry nodded. "Which is why I consult with you before any of my birthday adventures."

"So far, your couple matches have been spot-on."

"True, but having you confirm compatibility reassures me. I want everyone to live happily ever after."

"So do I." Her chest tightened, thinking after she matched her three clients she might not get the chance to do it again. Hadley loved what she did. "Where is the client located?"

"At the moment?" Henry glanced toward the doorway. "In the front lobby."

"Oh." That was unexpected. "I didn't realize you'd brought him with you."

"I've worked with you enough to know your process. Trust me, he doesn't want to waste a single moment."

A warning bell sounded in her head. She needed the client, but she didn't want to destroy her success rate. "Does he understand the search can't be rushed?"

"He's aware, and he's eager to get started." Henry pulled out his phone. "May I have him join us?"

Fallon had the kids this afternoon, so Hadley didn't have to be home right away. Henry was a friend who'd brought her several clients over the years. She trusted him.

She didn't enjoy being caught off guard with a pop-in potential client, but she needed to save her business. Rules had a place but so did practicality and common sense. "Yes, that's fine."

Henry tapped on his phone. "He'll be here shortly. Have I shared the latest photos of Noelle?"

Hadley oohed and aahed over the cute little girl.

The office line rang again. Maybe she should have

asked Ella to turn off the ringer before she left.

A door opened and then closed.

Henry grinned. "That must be him."

Hadley grabbed an empty folder from her desk drawer. When she looked up, a man stood in the doorway. Not just any man…

"Blaise?" She whispered his name, unsure if it was a plea or a question. "What are you doing here?"

Henry stood. "My work is done."

Hadley stared at Henry, who was walking around the desk toward her. "I don't understand."

"I'm just trying to help right a few wrongs. Hear him out. That's all I ask." Henry kissed her cheek. "I'll be in touch soon."

* * *

What are you doing here?

Blaise didn't answer Hadley's question. He couldn't because all he wanted to do was stare at her. She looked like he felt—awful. And that hurt because he was the one who'd caused them both so much pain.

He stepped into her office to let Henry exit.

Henry patted Blaise's shoulder. "Good luck."

Blaise would need more than luck. He needed a miracle.

Did he expect her to give him a second chance?

No.

293

Unlike his friends, who were sitting in the lobby to lend moral support after coming up with this multipronged plan, Blaise wasn't an optimist with matters of the heart. He had no experience. But his careless, thoughtless words had affected her business.

Whether or not she wanted anything to do with him personally, he would help save her company. An interview he'd given had gone live fifteen minutes ago. That was his first step to making sure Matched by Lowell survived. Because it wasn't only her livelihood at stake. Her sister, niece, and nephew depended on Hadley, too.

Eyes wide, she remained seated.

Slowly, he approached her desk. The tension in his shoulders made him want to slump, but he forced himself to stand straight. His gaze met hers. "I'm sorry, Hadley. I never meant to hurt you or your business. I'm doing what I can to make it right."

A beat passed and then another.

Hadley rested her clasped hands on the top of the desk. "There's nothing you can do to help me."

Her body language translated the words into what she really meant—*I don't want or need your help.*

Blaise understood, but he had to try. He would do whatever it took to make this right for her. "I didn't mean what I said on the video."

"You said what you believed in that moment." Her tone was cool and professional, but the quiver of her lower lip told him she was far from okay.

"Nothing can change that. The clients who left Matched by Lowell aren't coming back. They've canceled their contracts and been refunded their retainers."

That was worse than he thought. "I did an interview."

She didn't blink or show any emotion. "What does that have to do with me?"

"I answered questions about what I said on the video," he explained, wishing he could take credit for the next part. Offering an exclusive interview had been Brett's killing-two-birds idea. "I spoke with the reporter who I had a run-in with several weeks ago."

Her eyes widened. "The one you had a fight with?"

This wasn't the time to get caught up in semantics. "Yes. He wasn't the one who filmed us."

Hadley opened her mouth, but no words came out. She rubbed her forehead. "I guess that's something."

Her office phone rang.

"Do you need to get that?" he asked.

"No, it's more reporters. Probably looking for a statement about your interview."

"Not clients?"

Hope flared in her gaze but quickly died. "I spoke to the three earlier."

He flinched. "Only three?"

She nodded once.

Blaise felt nauseous. "Dash and Wes are quoted in the interview. Both praise your matchmaking abilities."

She inhaled slowly. "I'll thank them for that."

"I hope the interview helps. There are other things I will do." Blaise hated how the light in her eyes had dimmed. Worse was knowing he'd done that to her. "If we—"

"There is no we." Her tone was hard and hit him like a punch to the gut. "You made that clear in Las Vegas. You were pretending. That's all."

He hung his head with shame. Yes, he'd said that, but he hadn't meant it. "I was wrong. I was too upset to see what was right in front of my face."

Defiance in her eyes, she raised her chin. "What would that be?"

"You." The word seemed to hang in the air. "I didn't want to fall for you. I never planned on falling for anyone. Opening myself up the way I did. Allowing myself to be vulnerable. Hurt. Abandoned. I had enough of that with my mom and dad. But you. You broke through. You made me feel. Made me believe that I was worth more than my account balances. And then you chose Wes."

She didn't say a word, so he would keep going.

"I mean, you didn't choose Wes, but I thought you were picking him over me. The same way my parents picked heroin over me. And I lost it. Because even though I'm older now, and should be more mature, I'm still that little boy who wants someone to want him. To pick him over everything and everyone else. To make him feel like he's number one."

She blinked several times. "I don't know what to say."

"Then let me talk. I miss you, Hadley." Blaise poured his emotions into his words. "I can't take back what happened. I would if I could. But please understand how sorry I am. I don't care about the bet. But losing you has devastated me."

She closed her eyes. Exhaling, she opened them. "I was trying to do the right thing for your friend. I never meant to trigger a reaction from you. But what you said, how you reacted. Yes, we started off pretending, but I thought things changed pretty quickly. They did for me, so I broke the rules. I was happy to do that because I believed your feelings were the same as mine."

"Please. Let me make it up to you." He wasn't above begging. If she wanted him to grovel, he would. "Not just for your business. But you. I hate that I hurt you."

"Hurt?" Her gaze hardened and gleamed, cutting him to the core. "I'm heartbroken. I convinced myself you were different. That we had something special."

"We do." He didn't want to lose her. "If we can start over—"

"It's too late." The words, full of angst and sadness, tumbled out of her mouth. "I appreciate you doing the interview, and I hope it helps. But whether or not it does, I have to start over with my business. Save it. For myself and my family. That will take everything I have. There won't be anything left of me to give."

He stiffened. "What are you saying?"

"Goodbye." Hadley's voice shook. "I'm sorry you made a wasted trip to San Francisco. I know how valuable your time is."

He could barely breathe. "You're valuable to me."

She shook her head. "You'll find somebody else. Someone more convenient, who can give you the time you need and make you the priority you want to be in her life."

"I want you."

Her gaze locked on his. "Sometimes what we want isn't what we need."

His shoulders sagged. Logic told him to walk away because he'd lost.

"I understand." Blaise wasn't sure what he would say if he were standing in her shoes. "I won't stop trying to save Matched by Lowell."

Her face tightened, the lines around her mouth deepening. "Thank you."

He hated how cold her voice sounded when she was so warm, caring, and emotional. But he'd hurt her and now she was afraid to show that side of herself.

"So I guess this is it." Blaise spoke the words as much for his benefit as hers.

His heart was breaking because he'd imagined her in Portland with him. Not for a weekend or a week but for the rest of their lives. The three words "I love you" sat on the tip of his tongue, but he couldn't say those words. He fought off every instinct telling him to stay and fight. He hated to lose, but he saw no way to win this one.

"Goodbye, Hadley." He turned and left her office.

Chapter Eighteen

Goodbye Hadley.

Hadley held her breath. She sat frozen, waiting, each second passing as slow as a year. The click of the door closing sounded.

Silence.

Blaise was gone.

A jagged pain sliced through her. Her heart had been ripped from her chest, and each drop of blood squeezed out.

She couldn't believe he'd done an interview, let alone with the reporter who'd caused him so much trouble. That must have been difficult for him and to get his two friends involved…

The office line rang again. She waited for the call to go to voice mail, but the ringing continued. Unable to take hearing the sound any longer, she snatched the receiver. "Hadley Lowell."

"Hadley, it's Simone Winterhaven." The socialite's voice was syrupy sweet. "You refunded my retainer earlier today, but there's been a miscommunication. Perhaps your assistant misunderstood because I want to continue your services."

No mistake. No misunderstanding. Hadley had heard Simone's horrible message. The woman had threatened to condemn Matched by Lowell's services publicly if she wasn't refunded her money immediately.

What made Simone change her mind?

It made no sense.

And then the reason hit Hadley. "You saw Blaise's interview."

A beat passed. "I… Yes, I did."

Anger flared but so did relief. As emotions piled on top of each other, Hadley's control slipped. "I need to go. I'll be in touch."

She hung up before Simone could reply.

A sob welled deep inside Hadley. Blaise's interview might have worked, but…

Hearing him out had been a mistake. Hadley wanted to believe Blaise. She wanted him the same way he said he wanted her, but she was afraid.

A part of her had wanted to tell him to stay, but she hadn't. She couldn't believe things would get better between them because they never had for her in the past. That wasn't his fault or hers. It was just how her relationships turned out.

Letting him go this time hurt—oh, how it hurt—but the pain would be worse if they tried and then he left her again. And he would leave eventually because her other boyfriends had left after they'd gotten what they wanted.

Hot tears burned in her eyes.

She blinked once, twice, and then allowed the warm drops to fall down her cheeks. She covered her face with her hands and cried.

Yes, Hadley appreciated Blaise's efforts to help her business. She hadn't expected that, but…

Saying goodbye was the right choice.

The only option.

Doing the right thing sometimes hurt.

And this did.

As the tears flowed, she released the pain, the regret, and the memories. That would be the only way to push Blaise Mortenson from her mind and from her heart. At least she hoped that worked.

"Hadley?"

Her heart froze. Her breath stilled.

She lowered her hands to glance at the doorway.

Blaise stood with deep lines etched on his face. Worry clouded his gaze. Tears filled his eyes.

Oh, no. Her hands flailed, wiping the drops from her cheeks. If she'd known he was still here, she would've held herself together. She wouldn't have let herself lose control.

He came toward her, his steps purposeful, his gaze focused on her.

She cleared her dry throat. "I thought you left."

"I started to, but I couldn't."

"You hate losing."

"True, and I know you want me to walk away, but I can't. I won't." He went around the desk and stood next to her. "What we have is worth fighting for. I'll do whatever it takes to show you how much you mean to me."

She forced herself to breathe. "I…"

"Tell me what it'll take. I'll do anything."

Hadley fought to control her ragged breathing. "That's a dangerous thing to offer when you're a billionaire."

"Not when you're all I want. Need." He leaned against her desk, staring at her with an intensity that took her breath away. "I thought, if I won the bet, life would be perfect. I'd have more money, bragging rights, and be able to show everyone I belong. But nothing is perfect. Though, the two of us together comes close."

Words were easy to say. Actions… She squared her shoulders. "Tomorrow, you could change your mind."

"Not going to happen." His voice was strong and firm. "You're the only one for me. I'll spend today, tomorrow, and every day after that trying to convince you it's true."

"I want to believe you." Her voice cracked. "But I'm scared."

"So am I, sweetheart," he admitted. "I'm terrified. But you're worth feeling this way."

"Am I? Because I hate it." Hadley trembled, struggling for how to put her conflicting emotions into words. "I trusted you. Believed in you. In us. Now all I am is hurt and afraid."

He reached for her. "I'm…"

She shrugged off his hand. "I need to get this out."

Blaise nodded.

"Even if I forgive you and we make up, how do I know it won't happen again?" She sniffled, trying to hold herself together. "You hurt me. But what happened between us should have been a private moment. It wasn't. And that video is still out there. The person who filmed it is, too. There could be others waiting for the chance to do that. With you or us. And the thought of being exposed this way again…"

Her hands shook. She struggled to breathe.

"I can't change what I did or what the person with the camera did. I can't tell you someone else isn't out there lurking in the shadows. If I could, I would." His shoulders curled over his chest, but his gaze never wavered. "But I can promise you this. I will do better.

I never want to hurt you again. I want to protect you. I want to do what's best for you. Because when you walked away on Friday, you took my heart with you. I love you, Hadley."

She sucked in a breath, not sure she heard him correctly. "You love me?"

"I love you. You have no idea how much." He touched her shoulder only, this time she didn't shrug off his hand. "I don't want to live without you. Please give me a second chance. Let me show you how much you mean to me."

His words filled her with longing, but she still had doubts. "You and me. It's so complicated. We live in different states. Our businesses—"

"Aren't as important as us being together." He cupped her face. "I never thought I'd say that, let alone believe it, but you showed me it's true. You know my past. You know me. I've never wanted a family. Never thought I needed one. But that was the little boy who didn't want to deal with the reality of being abandoned again. What you have with Fallon and the kids… It's like a modern-day sitcom. Not perfect. But you love each other. Care about each other. I want to be a part of it with you and them."

Hadley fought the urge to lean into his touch. Heaven help her, but she wanted him to be a part of their family, too.

His Adam's apple bobbed. "If you tell me to go, I will, but you will remain in my heart forever, and I have a feeling I'll be in yours for at least a little longer."

The choice was hers. None of her planning or processes would help her. That meant doing the one thing she never thought she could do again—trust her heart.

Deep down, she knew, if she didn't give Blaise a second chance, she would regret it. Possibly for the rest of her life.

Being without him was difficult. A piece of her felt as if it had died on Friday night. But, if things ended between them again, at least Hadley would know she'd done everything in her power to be with him.

"I don't want you to go." She lowered his hand from her face, but laced her fingers with his. "I want you to stay with me."

"Always. We just need to work out the logistics."

"Shhh. Not now." She stood and kissed him on the lips. "We'll figure this out later."

"'This' meaning us?"

Joy overflowed from her heart. "Yes, us. I love you."

"I love you." Blaise flashed her a billion-dollar smile before releasing her hand. He removed something from his pocket and then knelt on one knee.

Her heart slammed against her rib cage. She covered her mouth with her hands.

"We haven't known each other long, but I want you to know I'm one hundred percent committed to you. To us. Once I realized that, waiting made no sense. There's no reason for us not to be together."

He opened the black velvet case and showed her the exquisite diamond, a big one, in a shiny platinum setting.

"Hadley Lowell, you match couples and help them find their happy endings. You are my perfect match. I want to spend every morning waking up to you and every night kissing you and dreaming about you. Will you marry me and live happily ever after?"

Tears of happiness filled her eyes. Her pulse raced, and she struggled to breathe. This was the last thing she expected, but it felt right.

"Yes!" Her voice cracked. "Yes, I'll marry you."

He kissed her hard on the lips, taking her breath away.

She leaned back. "But what about the bet?"

Blaise slid the ring onto her finger. "I don't care about the bet. Wes and Dash can battle it out. You're all I need. All I want." Blaise kissed her hand. "Hearing you say yes. Seeing my ring on your finger. That's all I need. I won something more valuable than the fund or the bragging rights. I get a future with you at my side. I couldn't ask for anything more."

Epilogue

November

Standing with the other wedding guests, Wes watched Blaise and Hadley dance for the first time as husband and wife. Joy radiated from their faces, a captivating mix of happiness and love with a dash of giddiness thrown in.

Ignoring the burning in his chest, Wes sipped from his champagne flute. He no longer drank much, but a wedding was a time of celebration—a time to splurge. Something he'd once done famously. Now…

He took another drink.

The bubbles tickled but in a good way. Excellent brand. It went down smoothly. Wes would need another glass. Maybe a few more.

Tonight would be a long one.

Not that he wanted to leave.

He couldn't imagine being anywhere else—wouldn't want to be.

Being Blaise's best man came with certain responsibilities, including making a thoughtful and funny toast, which he had, and not losing the rings before the ceremony, which he hadn't.

Except…

He was envious.

Jealous.

And it was eating him up inside.

Oh, he was on a first-name basis with those feelings in a way he'd never imagined being. And as friends do, they mocked and teased, poked and prodded, before laughing in your face.

Blaise kissed his pretty bride, and the crowd cheered.

Once upon a time, Wes believed he'd lived a charmed life. Everything he wanted had come to him ridiculously easy.

And then he got sick.

Suddenly *all* the things, the houses, and the unique, expensive toys didn't matter. His money could provide him with the finest medical care, but a six-billion-dollar net worth couldn't make him better. He'd been so jealous of his friends, healthy and happy and carefree, the way he'd once been. He would have traded places with them in an instant.

If only for a day.

And he shouldn't have felt that way.

Not when his friends had supported Wes in ways he never imagined, putting their lives and work on hold for him. But the bottom line had remained the same. He would have given up everything he owned, all the money in his bank accounts and investment portfolio, to be healthy—cancer-free.

Wondering if he would die before turning forty or even thirty-five sucked.

And cancer…

Remission.

You didn't win, sucker.

He downed his champagne before glancing around for the server carrying a tray of filled flutes.

"They look good together." Henry raised his glass in the bride and groom's direction and then took a sip. He'd paired an orange brocade tuxedo jacket with traditional black pants. On anyone else, the outfit would have been outrageous, but Henry easily pulled off the "seasonal color combination" as he called it. "Just as I thought they would."

Blaise spun Hadley, her white gown billowing, and then he dipped her. He brushed his lips over hers before continuing the dance.

Impressive. Wes had no idea Blaise could dance like that. But then again, Wes hadn't known everything he thought he knew about his friend. "Thought they would what?"

"Fall in love and get married. Though I pictured a Christmas or winter wedding, not an autumn-themed one, so my timing was off by a month or two. But I understand with her sister and the kids moving to Portland why they married so quickly." Henry watched the pair. "It's a good thing I don't want a job or I could give Hadley a run for her money with my mad matchmaking skills."

The man was too much.

Wes laughed. "Are you seriously taking credit for Blaise and Hadley getting together?"

"I am." Henry eyed Wes over the rim of his glass. "Blaise called her on my recommendation."

"To find me and Dash wives."

"That's what Blaise thought he was doing, but Hadley was what he needed in more ways than one." Mischief gleamed in Henry's eyes. "As we're seeing today."

Wes didn't like Henry's smugness. "How did you know what Blaise needed?"

"For a bunch of tech geniuses, you know little about people. Weren't you ever curious about his never mentioning his family or those bits and pieces of his past he told us?"

Not really, because Wes had been too busy living his own life. And that made him feel like a jerk. As Dash had said that night when Blaise told them about his past, this had been on them, too, for not being better friends.

Leave it to the bacchanalian billionaire, more of a man-child than the Wonderkid, to know what Blaise needed more than anyone else.

Wes sighed. "It won't happen again."

"Good." Henry appeared to scan the crowd. "And even though you and Blaise are close, I will be their child's godfather."

The certainty in Henry's voice made Wes laugh. "I suppose you had a role."

"A starring role," Henry reminded. "Though all of us played a part in their reconciliation."

"We did." Wes would never forget the eight of them in Blaise's hotel suite, brainstorming ways to get Hadley back until the wee hours of Sunday morning. Even Lex and Rizzo had taken part. After some sleep, they'd spent the day plotting and making contingency plans. Then, they'd gone ring shopping, which might have been funny if they hadn't been so on edge. He'd done the interview with Blaise and Dash before they'd all flown to San Francisco.

"Look at that delicious morsel." Henry winked at a beautiful woman with chestnut-colored curly hair standing on the opposite side of the dance floor. "I'll be getting her number before the end of the reception."

"Good luck." Though Henry never had trouble finding dates. Women loved his charm and eccentricities even if the guy never appeared serious about anyone. "Too bad you didn't join the bet or you could be in the running to win."

Henry shook his head. "I only make bets when I'm guaranteed to win."

Wes had heard about Henry rigging his birthday adventure that brought Brett and Laurel Matthews together. "You cheat to get the desired outcome."

"Cheat is such a negative word." Henry took another sip. "I prefer to say I enjoy giving fate a helping hand."

Wes snagged a full glass of champagne off a passing tray. "Looks like I'll be the one to win the bet. Dash brought Raina as his plus-one today."

Glancing at Dash and his date, Henry shook his head. "Spending time together doesn't guarantee falling in love. They get along well, but Dash will never propose to Raina. She invited herself to today's nuptials."

Wes stared at Henry in disbelief. "How do you know that?"

"I asked." A smug expression settled on Henry's face. "If I were a betting man, which I'm not, my money would be on Dash being the last man standing. No offense."

"None taken, but why?"

"It's simple," Henry said in a matter-of-fact tone. "Our beloved geek avoids conflict. He also hates change, so whatever woman hangs in there and asks him to marry her will end up his wife. But whoever that poor girl turns out to be, she'll need the patience of a saint to last that long."

Wes laughed. Henry's insight was on point. "That's why Dash is called Mr. Status Quo."

"Fits perfectly." Henry's gaze darkened. "So are you seeing any lovely lady or ladies?"

"No." Wes didn't want to discuss this, especially when Hadley and Blaise's happiness was making it difficult to breathe. "I'm taking a break from dating."

Wes hoped Henry didn't press for more information.

The song ended.

As Blaise stared at his bride on the dance floor, love poured from his gaze. Hadley's adoration for her groom was as palpable. Wes could feel it from where he stood.

"I love you," Blaise mouthed.

Hadley lit up. "I love you so much."

Wes's breathing hitched. His heart stilled.

I want that.

There'd been a time he'd never thought he'd be alive long enough to fall in love. Now wasn't the time. There was no one in his life—no one his heart wanted to pursue. And he wanted to do a few things first. But…

Someday.

Somehow.

Maybe he'd experience a taste of what his friends had found.

The beaming bride and giddy groom walked off

the dance floor.

"A break doesn't have to last long." Henry grinned, but the gleam in his eyes was more serious. "You may meet someone and change your mind."

Holding Hadley's hand, Blaise led his bride toward them. "Change your mind about what?"

"Love, marriage, and a happily ever after for Wes," Henry answered before Wes could. "And with a matchmaker in the group now, it'll be that much easier."

"I'm happy to help." As Hadley glanced at Wes, her smile softened. The interview had helped her business not only survive but also thrive. Still, she'd decided to downsize her client list, so she had more time for Blaise and her family. "Just tell me when you're ready."

The lump burning in Wes's throat kept him from answering. Instead, he nodded.

Blaise clapped his hand on Wes's shoulder and then lowered his arm. "Consider it our thank-you for an awesome best man speech and being a great friend who dragged me out of that club and helped me in Las Vegas."

Hadley rose on her tiptoes and kissed Wes's cheek. "Thank you."

Overcome with emotion, Wes took a drink.

Henry cleared his throat. "Don't forget who brought you together."

Hadley kissed Henry's cheek. "We'll never

forget."

"Good, because I need another godchild to spoil," Henry joked. "Little Henry or Henrietta has a nice ring to it."

Everyone laughed.

Blaise nudged Wes. "You can have godchild number two because we owe you."

"No, you don't." Wes loved his family, but Blaise and the others were his brothers by choice. His second family not connected by blood but as important to him. "Just keep the bet fund growing, so there's more to collect when I win."

Blaise laughed. "Dash might have something to say about that."

"He might." Especially given how unengaged Dash appeared to be as he danced with Raina. Time would tell. "But I'm in it to win it now that only two of us are still single."

"Just don't drink the water," Blaise cautioned.

"That worked well for you," Wes replied dryly. "I'm in no rush."

"You don't have to be." Blaise glanced at Hadley, and a smile lit up his face. Not that he wasn't glowing already. "As Wonderkid once told us, when you know you know. Even if the message takes time to sink in."

Hadley leaned against Blaise. "Did you tell him yet?"

Blaise shook his head. "So...there's going to be a bouquet and garter toss."

Wes's mouth gaped. "Wait. What? You hate those."

Blaise shrugged. "Hadley's niece and nephew wanted them, and I wasn't about to disappoint them. They love their uncle Blaise and think he's the coolest guy around. I won't aim for you, but Dash is free game. So is Henry."

"I heard that," Henry said.

"Leave it up to fate." Wes wasn't one to believe in tradition or magic, but... "Everyone deserves a shot at a happily ever after."

Maybe even him.

The Wish Maker
The Billionaires of Silicon Forest, Book Two

At Christmas, sometimes even impossible wishes come true...

One word changed Wes Lockhart's life forever. Cancer. Fighting for his life completely flipped his priorities, making him realize he wanted—no, needed—to use his billions to help others find the kind of second chance he'd been given. The first person he intended to help? The beautiful, kind, and dedicated oncologist who got him through his treatments and ushered him into remission. And what better time than the holidays to become her not-so-secret Santa?

Dr. Paige Regis has spent her entire career helping others, often at the expense of her personal life. She'd love to start a family of her own—but with her current patients and her plans to open a brand-new cancer center, it seems like an impossible dream. It's not until she reconnects with the charming Wes that she realizes he might just be the man to make all her Christmas wishes come true.

Can Wes and Paige open their hearts to the magic of the season—and each other—to get a shot at their very own Christmas miracle? Or will past hurts and doubts end their happily ever after before it even begins?

About The Author

USA Today bestselling author Melissa McClone has written over forty-five sweet contemporary romance novels. She lives in the Pacific Northwest with her husband, three children, two spoiled Norwegian Elkhounds, and cats who think they rule the house. They do!

If you'd like to find Melissa online:
www.melissamcclone.com
www.facebook.com/melissamcclonebooks
www.facebook.com/groups/McCloneTroopers
twitter.com/melissamcclone
www.instagram.com/melmcclone

Other Books
By Melissa Mcclone

STANDALONE

**A matchmaking aunt wants her nephew to
find love under the mistletoe…**
The Christmas Window

SERIES
**All series stories are standalone,
but past characters may reappear.**

The Billionaires of Silicon Forest
The Wife Finder
The Wish Maker

Quinn Valley Ranch
Relatives in a large family find love in Quinn Valley, Idaho…
Carter's Cowgirl
Summer Serenade

Beach Brides and Indigo Bay Sweet Romance Series
A mini-series within two multi-author series…
Jenny
Sweet Holiday Wishes
Sweet Beginnings

Her Royal Duty
Royal romances with charming princes and dreamy castles...
The Reluctant Princess
The Not-So-Perfect Princess
The Proper Princess

CPSIA information can be obtained
at www.ICGtesting.com
Printed in the USA
LVHW041156041119
636250LV00003B/520/P